Venetian Bind

by

Lawrence E. Rothstein

Cover Art by *Lea Schizas*

The Wild Rose Press, Inc.
PO Box 708
Adams Basin, NY 14410-0708
Visit us at www.thewildrosepress.com

Publishing History
First Edition, 2024
Trade Paperback ISBN978-1-5092-5415-6
Digital ISBN978-1-5092-5416-3

Published in the United States of America

Dedication

I would like to thank my wife, Jan, and my family for their constant support of my writing. Special thanks to C.N. Hetzner and Lois Patton for detailed comments, criticism, and inspiration. Thanks also to the members of several writing groups to which I have belonged for their encouragement and our sharing of ideas.

Prologue

The air resisted every breath. The stench of the steamy July stew of shit, piss, and death overpowered the nostrils. The gaunt form of Mordechai Croboda lay face down on the dirt floor next to the wooden planks that served as a bed. Bullets whizzed and whined inches above his head–the guards' daily fun. He heard the thud of a bullet ripping into flesh and the moan of a prisoner made an example of the futility of being Bosnian. The firing stopped abruptly. Not a typical day at the detention camp. Usually, there were several corpses to carry out.

Croboda slithered closer to another prisoner. "What's up?" he whispered.

"Saw some shiny black boots. Pakulić's thugs to round up prisoners and make 'em disappear," hissed the sweating prisoner. "Don't draw attention to yourself, Croboda. If they find out who you are, you're finished."

Too late. The jackboots headed his way. He considered running. A few poorly trained, sadistic misfits handled internal prison security. No need for tight security as the prison was surrounded by a minefield, open ground, and a company of Serbian troops. He'd play dumb and if the paramilitaries took him away through the minefield and the troops, he'd make his break later. In any case, with Sonja and Sasha both dead and his team smashed at Pakulić's hands, he little cared what happened to him if he could just take a few of Pakulić's bastards with him.

Croboda kept his head down until he was roughly pulled by his hair to a kneeling position. "That's him," said one of the paras, handing around a picture to his colleagues for confirmation. "We finally got the son-of-a-bitch. It'll be a pleasure to finish him."

"Damn!!! We have to take him back alive. Pakulić's orders. He wants to do him himself," said another black-shirted para. "But he didn't say the scum had to be in good condition," he smirked as he kicked Croboda in the ribs.

Croboda's face hit the dirt, and he lay still for a moment, trying to place the familiar voice of the last speaker. Another kick caught him in the jaw. The pain exploded in his head. He fought against blacking out as he was dragged to his feet. Wedged between two of the thugs, he was half dragged and half staggered out of the enclosure. The barracks were only a series of lean-tos with one open side so that the prisoners could always be seen. The captives would freeze to death in the winter–a system that was more cost-effective than the Nazi gas chambers.

There was no talking as the group, referring to a creased and stained map, slowly zigged and zagged through the minefield. When they reached the first troop checkpoint, the para leader handed over some papers and Croboda's picture. The Serbian sergeant signaled for them to wait. Just then, the pock-pock of small arms fire spurred the lounging troops to frenzied, confused action. They grabbed for helmets and weapons and ran for cover. In the commotion, the para leader and the familiar sounding kicker, pulled Croboda to the last checkpoint. The confusion had reached that spot as the whomp of mortar shells kicked up clouds of dirt and smoke.

The para commander on Croboda's left yelled to the franticly milling guards, "The sergeant's got our papers. He said to take our prisoner out here. We need to get him back to headquarters for questioning." There was only a nod as the sentries scrambled to take their fortified defensive positions awaiting the attack.

Once past the checkpoint, the familiar sounding para said to Croboda, "Now we run. Are you up to it?" Croboda realized that the voice was that of Shimon Bansky, a rabbi that Croboda had heard rallying Bosnian Jews to stay and fight the Serbs.

"Let's go," Croboda croaked through his swollen jaw.

****

For twelve days, the four wended a disjointed two-hundred-mile trek through heavily wooded areas, mostly at night. They talked little in order to avoid detection and conserve their energy. They camped without fires, drank from streams, and ate berries, wild mushrooms, and beef jerky. The least talkative of the men, Sachal, was a rabble-rousing Muslim cleric. He was all business on this mission as the point man scouting out the best concealed routes.

Croboda learned that the slim, dark-haired, mustachioed bogus para leader was Vladimir Strega, a hotelier, whose elegant hotel had been a center of Bosnian resistance activity until it was leveled by Serbian tanks. Strega had managed to escape through the city sewers. He had become a legendary phantom of the resistance, extracting heavily guarded Bosnian

3

leaders from supposedly impregnable fortresses.

Croboda asked whether the attack on the prison troops was a lucky coincidence or part of the plan. "Part of the plan, if you can call it a plan. There were only eight of us–the three of us who went into the camp and five who made as noisy an attack as possible. They were to keep the Serbs busy for as long as they could hold out," said Strega sadly. *More deaths to weigh on my conscience*, thought Croboda. *Why am I worth it?*

As if reading his mind, Bansky, the third member of the group, said, "We knew that Pakulić had sent men to find you. We had to get to you first and pull you out. We need you in Washington. With your work in Bosnia and your American contacts, you are the one to convince the West to intervene."

For the rest of the journey, the four men steered clear of war talk. Instead, each shared details of their favorite meals, imagination serving as a supplement to their meager fare. They parted company at Piran in Slovenia on the Gulf of Trieste. Croboda thanked his rescuers warmly and wished them luck, promising unconvincingly that he would contact them soon. As the rescuers headed back southeast toward Bosnia, a fishing boat smuggled Croboda across the Adriatic to Venice.

Croboda learned only after the war that Strega had emigrated to Venice. He heard that Bansky and Sachal had disappeared while trying to keep a death squad off of his trail. They were among the many fallen Bosnian patriots to whom Croboda owed his life.

Chapter 1

Marko Korb looked out across the Venetian lagoon as the sun was setting. His corpulent form was wedged into a padded dining room chair. Spread before him on the table was a feast of Venetian delicacies. The fried soft-shelled crabs looked succulent. The anchovy and garlic aroma of the sauce on the thick whole wheat pasta was tantalizing. He could smell the fragrant, sizzling Venetian specialty of the house, thinly sliced calves' liver and onions, being prepared in the kitchen by the noted hotel chef.

Korb was a gourmand and a gourmet. He should have been sampling and savoring these elegant dishes. But he couldn't. He thought of the last time he had gazed out at a sunset across the Venetian lagoon, entrance to the Grand Canal, and spotted a speedy launch preparing to depart.

The last time was in 1993, over twenty years ago. He had escaped from the Manjača Detention Camp in Banja Luka only to be pursued by Serbian death squads. Korb (or Croboda as he was then known) and his team of agents had been working undercover to provide Western countries and the UN with information concerning atrocities in order to encourage them to take more strenuous action against the Serbs. Stefan Pakulić, head of Serbian security in Bosnia, had sworn to kill Korb and sent his minions to the camp. They had missed him there due to the daring rescue, but managed to pursue him as far as Venice.

On that deceptively beautiful evening in 1993, Korb was about to board a launch that would take him to a small airport, then to Frankfurt, and finally to Washington for a high-level debriefing. A hail of bullets from the eastern shore of the lagoon killed the launch's crew and seriously wounded Korb. He now had one lung and still walked with a slight limp. Only a steely desire for vengeance and a lot of luck allowed Korb to escape that day. Along with his physical wounds, he carried with him the weight of the deaths of loved ones and colleagues who had made his work and his escape possible.

Korb diligently and successfully plied his contacts in Washington. The Western powers and the UN intervened more forcefully and an independent Bosnia was preserved. By the end of the war, however, Korb had tired of Washington and politics. Given his losses of friends and family in Bosnia, along with the disappointment in learning of Bosnian atrocities, he no longer wanted to return to his homeland. A Chicago businessman of Bosnian descent, whom he had met in DC, asked him to conduct a discreet inquiry into theft and sabotage at his pharmaceutical plant in Des Plaines. Korb accepted immediately.

The novice detective ferreted out a major opioid theft and smuggling scheme that had eluded both the FBI and the DEA. Oxycodone stamping machines had been tampered with so the tablets were slightly under the designated dosage. The excess opioid was siphoned off and collected by a mob-connected Russian *émigré* cleaning crew and smuggled into Eastern Europe by a complex chain of shippers and importers.

Not only did Korb lay out the whole operation to federal authorities, he used their embarrassment at being scooped by an inexperienced private investigator to keep the name of his client's company out of press releases and public court documents for over three years. He was also able to show the feds that the same nefarious scheme was being carried out at several drug companies in the Chicago area and possibly nationwide.

The drug execs were grateful and impressed. Korb's reputation as a top-notch investigator grew rapidly. The fat checks he received furthered his business and his liking for Chicago.

Now, twenty years later, he was once more gazing at the lagoon and contemplating a death. This time it was Stefan Pakulić who was dead, murdered on a Venice back street and tossed into a canal. "Sewage to sewage," Korb mouthed silently. The now-renowned investigator had been brought to Venice to assist in the homicide investigation.

Why had he come? Mostly to ensure that his nemesis was really dead. Should he help with the investigation? Whoever killed Pakulić–that monster— had done Marko Korb and the world a favor. Pakulić was a war criminal and the cursed target of many Bosnian families who had lost dear ones to his reign of terror. Why couldn't the Bosnian war hero accept this gift and finally close out a dark chapter of his life? He had promised his diligent and protective, young associate, Kelan Su, that they would return to their pending cases in Chicago after identifying the body. Rather than feeling relieved of a gnawing obsession by the Serbian's death, Korb felt empty, incomplete.

The detective knew that he was the most able person to profile both Pakulić and his killer. The victim Korb knew intimately and the shooter he likely was acquainted with or at least understood what impelled her or him to do it. The Bosnian community in Venice was insular. They wouldn't talk to the police, but they might talk to him. In fact, the detective had received anonymous feelers, apparently from Bosnians in Venice, urging him to come. How they had heard of the Venice police request was unknown. But they were clearly afraid of two things: What Pakulić had been planning, and who the Italian authorities were likely to blame for the Serbian beast's murder. These fears increased Korb's feeling of obligation to investigate.

Korb had a reputation to maintain. A substantial number of the world's largest corporations were on his client list. The brilliant investigator had been consulted on thorny cases by police agencies from Interpol to Scotland Yard to the FBI. He had also tangled with some of them and come out on top. Korb's ego was as swollen as his body. Korb knew but also felt that it must continually be proved that he was the smartest investigator in the world when it came to flushing out secrets and identifying human foibles and their criminal results.

The telephone rang and was brought to him by his associate, Su. Korb put the receiver to his ear and said, "Yes, Inspector, this is Korb." A brief pause and then, "Thank you. The accommodations are more than adequate and the chef is a magician." Another momentary pause as Korb, listening, pursed his lips and shut his eyes. "Yes, Inspector, you may send the boat for me tomorrow at ten. I am at your service." He looked up as an audible sigh escaped Su's lips accompanied by her darkening, disappointed look. "Well, Kelan, how is your Serbo-Croatian?" he said.

Chapter 2

KELAN SU

Korb despised legwork. He always left the fieldwork to me. Although my Italian was very good thanks to a study abroad opportunity and two visits to Italy, my Serbo-Croatian was non-existent. Korb would have to go out and question people. I shuddered at the thought of him negotiating his 350 pounds onto *vaporettos* and water taxis! Furthermore, I was responsible for his security–difficult enough in the States where I was familiar with the territory and his many enemies and allies. The Chicago townhouse where we lived and worked was a veritable fortress. We also had Desmond St. Clair, a former Brit SAS commando and cyber security expert, to provide help with protection along with superb chef and valet services. Here I was a fish out of water. I would have to broach the subject of security with Inspector Mazzini when we met with him in the morning. For the moment, I would have to learn what I could from my boss about the expat community. He was not used to reporting to me—it was generally the other way around.

What profoundly worried me now was that Korb's emotions were tied up in this case. A recipe for disaster. What made him the genius I admired was his ability to approach the most emotionally complex matters coldly and intellectually. Further, he shunned cases where plodding, but thorough, police work was required. I would put my money on the Venice police and the *carabinieri* eventually finding the killer by plumbing the local Bosnian expat community. What was Korb trying to prove?

For that matter, what was I trying to prove? Why am I working for Korb? Isn't he a mercenary, a hired gun, for some of those same corporate and governmental powers that tormented my parents? Am I simply rationalizing when I see him as a quixotic crusader for justice and me as his Sancho? Isn't he as intolerant of failure as my parents? Doesn't he, as my parents, prefer not to see that I am a woman? I want, I *need*, to feel that I am a woman while fighting the good fight. I need the approval of someone I respect. Am I a fool to look to Korb and his work for this? My parents certainly think so.

That train of thought morphed into: What have I done with my life? And what about my parents? They came to America with nothing. They left their families behind. They slaved and scrimped to make a go of a small grocery store. They weathered crooked suppliers, frequent robberies at gunpoint, a continuously declining neighborhood, racial hostilities and the onslaught of the big box chains. We lost my brother in the process–hit by a car as he chased two ten-year-old kids out of the store after their bungled attempt at theft. He had a twenty-dollar bill in his hand. I think he wanted to give it to them. You'd think the kids would have kept running. Nope. They turned back to help him.

After my brother's death, everything my parents had that wasn't tied up in the business went to me. They ate warmed-over rice and vegetables too old to sell, while I dined on shrimp, beef, and chicken freshly cooked with loving care and crustless lunch sandwiches of Boar's Head deli meats. They sent me to private schools, to the University of Chicago, and finally to Harvard Law. They were proud when I graduated U of C with a 4.0, but were disappointed when I was only fourth in my class at Harvard Law. All the hopes and desires they may have had for my brother were channeled to me. They forgot that I was coming of age as a young woman. Trying to please them, I forgot it too.

It crushed them when I told them I was joining the Chicago police force. "What kind of job is that for a Harvard-educated lawyer with job offers from federal judges and top law firms?" they asked. I told them I owed it to my brother, those two kids, and people like them struggling to get by. They were the ones I would "serve and protect." A foolish hope as I soon realized and felt guilty that I had let them down once again. They would never understand that I couldn't take those seemingly plum jobs. Yet it was their fights against injustice and overwhelming economic forces that drove me to the choices I made.

Pushing aside these bitter thoughts, I looked out to the lagoon and into a backdrop of spires and cupolas. The one bright spot in this whole venture was that I loved Venice. It was a fairyland. The canals, buildings, bridges, islands, and little neighborhoods were a feast of serendipitous wonder. As there were no automobiles, people on foot and in water transports were constantly in neighborly contact. There were drawbacks to the ubiquitous proximity of other people. Privacy disappeared. Gossip was the common currency. Foreigners and tourists were readily identified. These could be advantages rather than drawbacks to a detective. I was counting on it.

Chapter 3

With some help from Su and a uniformed officer, Korb managed the two steps into the police patrol boat. He sat gingerly, with a look of distaste, in the plastic cockpit chair. Since that last time on the lagoon, the detective hated boats. There was no place he felt less secure. As the obese man tried to grip the sides of the seat that his immense derriere overlapped, the craft sped across the lagoon and down the Grand Canal, under the Rialto Bridge, past Piazza San Marko to the Castello sestiere, one of the six districts that made up Venice. Standing behind Korb, Su, who had been a Chicago cop for four years, compared notes with a young officer about city police work.

Police headquarters was in a former Benedictine Abbey at Campo San Zaccaria. Rumor had it that the Abbey was a favorite trysting place of Casanova. He wouldn't like it now. Despite a noble façade, the interior of the building looked like every big city police headquarters–dingy, in need of paint and polish, and furnished in surplus. Ramshackle cubicles were filled with seedy, worried characters–some police, some "customers." Korb hated the stink of despair that hung over such places.

Inspector Mazzini's office was not much of an improvement, although it had a window overlooking a side canal and a small cobblestone bridge. Mazzini stood and smiled as Korb and Su were ushered in by a crisply saluting, uniformed officer.

"So good to finally meet you, Signor Korb," said Mazzini, vigorously shaking the famous detective's flabby, but strong, hand. "Signorina Su, it is a very great pleasure to meet you as well." The smile on his finely chiseled features brightened as he took her hand and looked her over in that appreciative and sexy manner that seemed to be instilled in Italian men from birth. "Please, sit down. Would you like an espresso?" Both his visitors shook their heads.

"Let's get down to business, Inspector," said Korb impatiently. "This is very distasteful to me. I can't say I am sorry that Pakulić is dead, or that I would like to see his killer in jail. But I have agreed to help and I will. Please fill us in on the investigation so far."

Mazzini explained that Pakulić had been found floating in the Canale di Cannaregio near Campo San Geremia. He had been shot in the head at close range and either fell or pushed into the canal. No exit wound.

"The time of death?" Korb interrupted.

"Between two a.m. and three a.m. on Sunday morning, 11 May 2014. At approximately one-fifty-five he was seen leaving the casino at the Palazzo Vendramin-Calergi with at least three other people. We haven't yet been able to identify the others. It's about a ten-minute walk to the place where the body was found. Residents along the Rio Terra San Leonardo, a walkway that leads from the casino to the scene of the crime, thought they heard two shots around two-thirty. A water taxi driver returning to the depot saw the body floating at three and called the police."

Su scribbled feverishly in her notebook. Mazzini

paused to be sure his audience was still following his exposition. Watching Su, he raised his eyebrows in a question to Korb.

"Not to worry. She has an almost photographic memory, but it reassures her to have written notes. Please continue, Inspector."

Su looked up at Mazzini with a sheepish smile.

Reassured, the Inspector went on, "There was not much current or traffic in the canal that night. The body would have stayed pretty much where it landed. Police divers found a gun—a Walther P22, small caliber pistol. It was found not far from the body at the bottom of the canal. Serial number filed away. No fingerprints or other trace evidence. Because it was in the water, the techs couldn't tell if it had been recently fired. The gun had not been in the canal long. Slugs matched the one in the body as to make and caliber. We don't put much stock in ballistics markings, especially with the battering of the slug recovered from the victim. Two shell casings were found. My men are still searching the scene. If the weapon had started with a full clip and one in the chamber, two shots were fired."

Mazzini surveyed his audience again. Korb nodded, indicating that he should go on.

"The Rio Terra della Maddalena, which is behind the casino, is a hangout of prostitutes looking to hook up with winning gamblers. Pakulić was a predator who frequented and brutalized hookers, particularly those of Bosnian extraction."

Su frowned, pen poised in the air. The Inspector glanced at her, hesitated, and then went on.

"There are quite a few Bosnian prostitutes in the Cannaregio. The Bosnian community is poor, having lost everything in the war even though the war ended almost twenty years ago. A lot of the young girls end up as whores. Some of the more well-off members of that community operate seedy hotels on the Lista di Spagna where the prostitutes take their clients. The site of the murder is on the way to this area. We hauled in and interrogated the streetwalkers in the area. No one saw anything. There's a code of silence. There was similar stonewalling from the expat community. That's it," Mazzini concluded.

Korb nodded. "A very efficient summary, Inspector. Did you get all of it, Kelan?"

"Yes, sir," she said.

"Any questions?" her boss asked.

Su hesitated. "Well, I would like to know what Pakulić had been up to in Venice besides picking up prostitutes. What do your sources say, Inspector? I take it he doesn't live here permanently."

"Ahhh," drawled the Inspector. "That's where things get interesting. Pakulić has been talking to Italian neo-fascists. They hang out at the Soledoro, a *carnevale* mask shop in the Dorsoduro sestiere. Our contacts in the intelligence community think they are planning an action against Muslims in Italy, some of whom are Bosnian."

"Inspector," broke in Korb, "I will need a police launch, a driver, and a plainclothes officer at my disposal."

Mazzini nodded. "You may have the craft and driver you came with and Detective Campari will assist you. Anything else?"

"The names, addresses, and statements of any persons interviewed by your officers, the officers' reports, and anything you have or can obtain on Pakulić's whereabouts since his arrival in Venice, and on the fascists in Venice and the Bosnian expat community," added Korb.

Mazzini shook his head and chuckled slightly. He knew the gargantuan detective would be demanding.

The Inspector handed Korb a thick file folder, which he immediately passed to Su who opened it and perused the contents. "Looks like what we need, Chief," she said.

Korb glared. He considered sobriquets like "Chief" or "boss" flip familiarities.

"Satisfactory. That will be all for the time being, Inspector. If anything else comes up, we'll let you know. *Arrivederci*." With a grunt, Korb heaved his bulk out of the chair.

Mazzini and Su also stood. The Italian shook Korb's and Su's hands and showed them to the door. The Inspector nodded to the officer who had shown his two visitors in. The young policewoman escorted the pair out through the maze of desks and cubicles.

Mazzini, alone in his office, shook his head. He was stunned by the abrupt departure of the two detectives. His face screwed up in a wry smile. *Well, Korb really lives up to his "no-nonsense" billing. I just hope he also lives up to his reputation for success. Buona fortuna.*

Chapter 4

KELAN SU

Detective Angela Campari met us at the boat dock. Korb was clearly taken aback. He was uncomfortable with women. Except me, that is. I guess he really didn't think of me as a woman, more as an extra appendage. Detective Campari introduced herself and said she was thoroughly briefed on the material in the file. Her orders were to assist us in every possible way and to provide liaison with the Venetian police. Korb seemed assuaged by her forthright and efficient manner and regained his composure after the first stumbling acknowledgment of her presence.

She not only sounded efficient but looked so, with her trim, petite figure neatly encased in a finely cut business suit. Italian tailors are miracle workers. I'd have to ask her who her tailor was. I usually wore black, sometimes white. Today it was black slacks, a white silk camisole, and a black blazer. Blah, blah, blah. But I loved my shoes. Running shoes with soft black suede uppers, custom-made for me by New Balance. They looked like Capezio dancing shoes, but felt like suede gloves. No heels. Don't need 'em at six feet. Working my toes in those velvety, sensuous concoctions was almost better than an orgasm. Well, not really, but I hadn't had many opportunities to make that comparison. A strictly raised, Asian-American woman who is tall, a martial arts expert, Harvard law school grad, former Chicago cop, and live-in assistant to an eccentric and demanding world-famous detective seems to intimidate most men, except for the jerks who think such a conquest will raise their macho creds.

"What's our plan of action?" I asked in Italian for Campari's benefit.

Korb responded in fluent Italian. Campari and I were to visit the shops near the Soledoro, keep an eye on who was going in or out, and enter the mask shop and browse for as long as possible without arousing suspicion. "Try talking to the owner and clerks, but ask no pointed questions. Are you armed?" he asked Campari.

"Certainly!" she replied in unaccented English.

I didn't like guns although, as a police officer, I was well-trained in using them. They were messy, liable to injure innocents, and too easily fell into the wrong hands. They were sometimes good for intimidation, but they really destroyed the line of my clothing. I relied on street smarts and martial arts to protect Korb and myself.

"What will you be doing?" I asked Korb.

"Officer Treu and I will be going to the Cannaregio to speak to Bosnian expats. We'll drop you in the Dorsoduro. Keep in touch with me every hour by cell phone," instructed Korb.

I didn't like leaving him on his own, but had to admit that this was a good use of our resources.

Campari whispered in my ear, "Is he always this imperious?" An exhaled "Ha!!!" escaped me. I whispered, "Y' ain't seen nothin' yet." Campari looked at me quizzically and then, with my meaning dawning, nodded her comprehension.

"Of course," said Korb as he approached the boat, "we can't do all of this without lunch." He never missed a meal. "What do you think of Ai Tre Spiedi, Detective Campari? I am dying to try the braised eel and polenta," the fat detective said, the light dancing in his usually cool blue eyes. When he thought of an excellent meal, that man was almost childlike despite his three chins, slicked-back, thinning gray hair and massive, double-breasted, pin-striped suit.

Campari nodded appreciatively. "A delightful setting and superb food. I thought it was something of a secret among native Venetians," she said. "I love the grilled *orata*." Campari, like most Venetians, had a deep appreciation for local seafood. I would love to try these delicacies too, but I was impatient to get the investigation moving and finished. It irked me that the apparently all-business Campari warmed to the lunch idea so quickly.

I guided my boss to his now customary seat on the launch. He sat down warily. However, his delighted contemplation of the braised eel and polenta dish awaiting him seemed to lessen his fear of the water. Standing behind him, I enjoyed the wind in my hair.

Treu expertly drove the powerful motorboat, quickly passing under the Accademia Bridge and along the Grand Canal. Soon, we were tied up at the restaurant, greeted by a solicitous proprietor awestruck at meeting the storied Marko Korb. In the cloistered life of Venice, the news of the renowned investigator's arrival and possibly of his mission had traveled like lightning.

****

As our quartet left the restaurant after an elegant repast, another distraction came into view. The restaurant was adjacent to the lacey, pink and white, fifteenth-century, Ca d'Oro, an exquisite ducal palace containing Baron Franchetti's fabulous private art collection, which had been given to Venice after World War I. It was difficult to decide whether the fantastic carved stone and marble building or the superb collection of paintings and statuary were the main attractions.

Korb explained that Franchetti had amassed Titians, Carpaccios, and, in a special niche, Mantegna's mannerist *St. Sebastian*, bound and pierced with arrows, looking heavenward. "I am especially fond of the Latin inscription on the ribbon at the bottom left of the painting which reads: 'Nothing is stable if not divine. The rest is smoke.'

"We must stop in. But not now. We have our own smoke to clear away."

Chapter 5

After Su and Campari disembarked in the
Dorsoduro near the Accademia Bridge, Korb and Treu
backtracked to the Cannaregio. "I will be visiting an old
Bosnian acquaintance of mine," he told Treu. "Head
toward the Rialto Bridge. He owns the Albergo Ponte e
Palazzo on Strada Nuova. His apartment is there." Treu
nodded and guided the craft in that direction. When
they arrived at the nearest docking place, Treu assisted
Korb from the boat.

"Shall I go with you?" he asked.

"No. Bosnian expatriates are wary of the police,
and the discussion will be in Serbo-Croatian. Wait here
for me." Korb recalled something. "Oh, would you
please fetch my walking stick? I left it under the seat of
the launch."

Treu nodded curtly and turned on his heel toward
the boat. He was annoyed at being left out of the action
and being treated like a mere chauffeur. Treu found the
ebony cane with the golden crouching lion on the
handle. As he grasped it, he noticed that it had a nice
heft. *Might be useful in a fight*, he thought. He brought
it to Korb.

The detective took the stick, thanked the officer,
and said, "I was just thinking it might be good if you
took a look at the crime scene while I am talking with
my friend. It's two streets up from here. I know the

Lawrence E. Rothstein

techs have been over it carefully, but there is always the possibility that in observing the scene something will occur to you that others have missed. Check out the buildings that have a good view of the canal. I'll meet you back here in about an hour."

With his feathers less ruffled, Treu nodded to Korb and turned to go up the street. The detective watched him go with a slight smile on his face. He tapped his cane twice on the ground and started toward the hotel's entrance. The large man tapped up four marble steps to the brocaded, darkened lobby of the hotel. At the front desk, he addressed the bow-tied, blue-blazered clerk, "*Buongiorno. Signor Korb a vedere Signor Strega. Il m'aspetta.*"

"Ah, yes, Signor Korb. The elevator is on your left. Signor Strega's apartment is on the fifth floor," said the clerk. As the detective entered the elevator, the uniformed operator nodded to him. The large passenger said, "*Cinque, per favore.*" The operator closed the grille and the outer door closed automatically. The creaky elevator seemed to wheeze and strain at Korb's bulk.

On the fifth floor, it stopped with a slight recoil. The operator opened the grille and the outer door slid open. Korb was looking at a small marble hallway with two doorways. As he exited the lift, an ornamental set of double doors opened at the opposite end of the hallway.

"Won't you come in, Marko? It's been a long time," said Strega, extending his hand, which Korb grasped and shook firmly. Strega stood aside and ushered Korb in with a slight bow.

Vladimir Strega was sixtyish, tall, lean, and

24

slightly stooped. His hair and goatee were white. Korb noticed wistfully that time and the burdens of deep loss had greatly changed the handsome, dashing phantom of the resistance much as it had changed the intense, athletic, idealistic, slim Mordechai Croboda into the obese, detached, egotistical Marko Korb.

Korb stepped into a black-and-white marble foyer. It looked like an art deco movie set—large white urns in niches and modern chandeliers with metallic concentric circles hanging by three chains from the two-story atrial ceiling with a round skylight. It was not what he expected after seeing the classic, but shabby, sixteenth-century Venetian decor of the lobby.

Strega noticed Korb's appraising survey of the foyer. "Do you like it?" he asked. "It really was my daughter's idea." The clever detective read Strega's demeanor as saying that he did not like it himself but was very anxious that others should like it as a tribute to his daughter's taste.

"Very nice," said Korb unenthusiastically.

"Let's talk in my study." Strega signaled to a maid entering the foyer. He opened a door on the left and led Korb into his inner sanctum, a large room with oriental rugs on the floor, walls lined with book shelves, and worn dark leather furniture. The hotelier motioned to a chair and Korb slowly lowered his bulk into it. "I suppose you've not come to renew our acquaintance, but to talk about Pakulić," said Strega with a slight smile.

"You're right, of course, Vlado. In truth, our acquaintance is wrapped up with a time too painful to recall. I'm here to find Pakulić's killer and possibly exorcise some of my demons," said Korb, frowning and shaking his head. "What can you tell me about him?"

"You knew the extent of his depravity in Bosnia. It got worse. He's been involved in torture, assassinations, and drug smuggling with neo-fascist groups across Europe. He also likes, *liked*, to beat up prostitutes and has probably murdered a few," said Strega, grimacing. "He went in for high stakes poker at the casino here in Venice. Lost regularly, but always returned the next night with more money. Rumor has it that the money was paid to him by the Italian section of Golden Dawn to organize an anti-immigrant riot. I heard that he failed to deliver what he promised and the neo-fascist bastards were angry."

"So you think that the Golden Dawn might be responsible for his murder?" said Korb.

"Why not?" said Strega with a shrug. "Pakulić was becoming a liability. His dissolution was increasing. He was no longer reliable." Strega abruptly stopped speaking as the maid entered with a coffee service on a tray. He indicated the desk with a nod. The maid placed the tray there and left the room silently. His former rescuer poured and handed Korb a cup.

Korb accepted the cup and shook off the offer of sugar. "We are looking into the neo-fascist angle. I gather they hang out at a mask shop called Soledoro. Do you have any names?"

"Keep an eye on Fabio Porello and Tiziano Massimo. Porello's what passes for brains behind the organization in Venice and Massimo is the chief enforcer. They're both brutes."

Korb pursed his lips silently for a moment, fixing the names in his memory and thinking of how to move to a touchier subject. "The problem I see is that this did not seem like a professional hit–one missed shot, only one on target, brass left on the scene. Vladimir, what about the Bosnian community? We both know there are plenty of people here who wanted to see Pakulić dead and would have loved to pull the trigger."

"Of course, Marko, and I am one of them. However, I haven't heard about any involvement of our people and I surely would have. We are a tight community and can keep few secrets from each other." Strega gave his interrogator a straight, hard look.

Korb shook his head slowly. "And you wouldn't tell me if you had heard one of your people did it," he said with a knowing smile. Strega simply nodded.

"Vladimir, where were you between two a.m. and three a.m. on the morning of the murder?" Korb asked abruptly.

"I was here all night except for a brief excursion around the neighborhood to walk the dog."

"Did you see anyone or anything unusual while you were out?"

"No, nothing unusual." Strega went on. "But you must know that this neighborhood is active even in the wee hours. There were people around. I didn't see anyone unusual, or anyone I knew for that matter. I am surprised that no one saw the murder take place, but that street is unlit and just off the beaten path."

"Was your daughter here with you all night?"

"Yes. She came home from work at seven. We dined together. I had made a *salade nicoise*. We watched some television. She went to bed around midnight. I stayed up and read until about two a.m. when I went out to walk the dog."

"Do you usually walk the dog at that hour?"

"No, my daughter usually walks him around midnight. But she was tired and the dog was dozing, so I said I'd take him out later," said Strega with a nervous twitch of his mustache.

The detective pressed on, "Do you often walk the dog at night?

"No."

Korb was getting curious. "I would like to speak with your daughter, if I may. Is she here?"

"No, I'm afraid not," responded Strega, shifting his glance from the large man to the door.

"Would you ask her to call me at this number when she gets in?" said Korb, handing Strega a card. "I must be going, but I will be in touch with you again soon. I will need the names and contact information for any Bosnian expats who live in this area. If you think of anything else, please call me at the number on the card." Korb smiled. "It was good to see you again, my friend. I hope we can soon put all of this behind us."

With that, Korb rose, leaning on his cane. He came over to Strega as he was starting to rise and said, "No need to get up. I can find my way out. Thank you for speaking with me." Korb added gravely, "Vladimir, know that I will do my best to protect you and yours, but I *will* get to the bottom of this. It would be wise if you and your daughter were frank with me."

Half risen, Strega collapsed back into his chair and looked at his friend almost pleadingly. Korb gave Strega a not unsympathetic look and turned abruptly to leave the room.

Chapter 6

KELAN SU

By the time we disembarked near the train station in the Dorsoduro, Angela and I were on a first name basis. I was curious about why she became a cop, so I asked her.

"Not very surprising," she replied. "I come from a police family–my father, two uncles, two cousins, and my brother are all cops."

"Did they encourage you to join the force?"

"Just the opposite. They tried to talk me out of it. There is still a macho bias."

"No kidding," I said with a tight-lipped smile. "So how come you stuck with it?"

"I worshipped my older brother. I wanted to do everything he did. When he joined the force, I knew I would have to do the same. Once my dad and uncles recognized the inevitability of my becoming a cop, they helped me get in good with the local commanders."

"Mazzini?"

"Oh yeah. He and my Uncle Tomaso are best friends and former partners. Not to mention that Mazzini has an eye for the ladies. Doesn't mind having a young, good-looking woman to order around. I try to keep him at bay without busting his balls. I think he's slowly starting to respect me as a detective. At least he's given me some plum assignments."

"You seem to handle the *machismo* better than me," I said with a wistful smile.

"Is that why you quit the force?" Angela sounded as curious as I had been about her joining up.

"Partly. I was tired of the Asian-American woman stereotype. I was advanced quickly to detective, but endured all the usual assignments with community relations between the Chinese and Vietnamese communities and the Asian gang task force."

"How about your commanders? Did they hit on you?" Angela asked.

"No. They were oh sooo condescendingly liberal, pushing me career wise, while distancing themselves personally for fear of being seen as sexually interested. But the sly hostility of the other detectives didn't stop them from hitting on me." I felt my face twist into a grimace. Thinking about it still fired those angry, raw nerves in the pit of my stomach.

"Sounds like you faced a lot more hostility than I did. Of course, I had family to smooth the way," said Angela, widening her eyes in a sympathetic smile.

"Yeah, but it wasn't just that. The straw that finally broke this camel's back occurred with the gang task force." Clearly, Angela was super at drawing people out. I liked her and trusted her. I said, "I'm about to tell you a story that I have never had the heart to tell anyone."

Angela cocked her head to the right and leaned forward slightly, showing both concern and interest. "Go on."

"My partner, Les Treadwell, was a ten-year veteran. Thought he was a hotshot crime fighter. He wasn't really interested in law enforcement or investigation. Just wanted to get the scum, generally meaning non-white gang members, off the streets any way he could. If he scored some coke or a few bucks of drug money, those were the perks of the job."

"I get the picture," said Angela nodding her head in agreement. "I have to say that Italian cops are less racist but more venal. They aren't cowboys. They don't see their role as 'cleaning up the streets.' All they want to do is to keep a modicum of order and satisfy the higher-ups. Many take bribes, not so much for protecting criminal enterprises, but simply for pursuing legitimate complaints or ignoring the minor crimes of generally law-abiding citizens."

"Aren't there many on the payroll of organized crime? That's one of our big problems," I asked.

"Not really. Italian cops are simply too afraid or too pessimistic to pursue organized crime vigorously. There are rare actions against the mafia undertaken by left-wing examining magistrates and prosecutors with hand-picked staff. Short-lived describes both the successes and often the officials," Angela added. "Get back to your story. What happened with your partner that drove you off the force?"

"Yeah. He also thought he was god's gift to women. I knew there'd be trouble between us. For six months, I took his racist and sexist comments and ignored the violations of police regs. Nothing major, although I suspected some of our collars included planted evidence."

I went on. "But one hot summer afternoon, we were pursuing the tip of a, to my mind, unreliable informant, a junkie and drug dealer who was protecting

Lawrence E. Rothstein

his turf by ratting out a competitor. Les and I pulled up to two men on a street corner in a poor Asian neighborhood. Les, from the passenger side, opened the door smack into one of the men, a tall, skinny, black man holding a brown paper bag. He had been talking to a Vietnamese twenty-something. As the black man staggered back from the door, Les leapt out, drawing his service weapon. He yelled some stupid TV cop show shit like 'Freeze scumbag!' Both men ran, and we chased them down an alley that went under the expressway."

"Wow. You sure have the details down. When was all this?" asked Angela, her eyes wide.

"About four years ago. But I don't think I'll ever be able to forget it," I said with the bitter taste of gall in my mouth.

"Well, sometimes talking about things can help you get past them," she said. "Please go on."

"Okay. The alley they were running down was blocked by a tall, razor-wired cyclone fence. The men attempted to climb it. Les yelled at them to halt. They turned to face us. It seemed like in slow motion. The black man's jacket had caught in the fence. As he reached behind him to free it, Les screamed, 'You son-of-a-bitch' and fired twice. A hole appeared in the man's gut, spouting blood. Les sneered at me and hissed, 'Fire your piece. Don't matter if you hit nothing.' I wouldn't do it.

"Les searched the fallen man for a weapon. Didn't seem to find one. I checked the man's pulse, which was very weak, and called for an ambulance. As I called, Les moved between me and the man. I heard a metallic clatter. Les said, 'OK. There it is. It's under him.' He held up a gun. I knew Les had a gun in his ankle holster, but I couldn't say this one was his."

Angela shook her head. "Of course, I've heard of such things. There are not many police shootings here and handguns are hard to come by. But I've certainly had to keep my mouth shut about a lot of violations of procedure. I see it as a work requirement. If you don't generally support your fellow officers, they'll see that you can't do your job. But this Les seems like a real piece of shit."

"You'd better believe it! At the cop house, Les wanted me to back up his story, but all I was willing to say was that I could not see whether or not the man had drawn a weapon. When the man died, it was Les who relayed the news to me with a smirk. I think even our superiors were getting fed up with Les. He was suspended, but only for a month. After that, no one wanted to partner with me. The young cop assigned to do it told me he had protested the assignment because he felt he couldn't trust me. Would you believe it? Trust me?!!! I couldn't accept that my integrity was in question because I wouldn't back up the lies of a corrupt cop. I resigned. Everyone breathed a sigh of relief."

I felt empty. My eyes burned with tears. My neck seemed too weak to hold my head up. Yet in the pit of my stomach, there was a fluttery feeling–an anticipation of something hopeful opening its fragile petals after a long winter of dormancy. After all, I was now working with someone for whom I had a deep respect.

Angela looked at me and shook her head sadly. I could tell there was some conflict in her attitude toward what I had told her. She was a good cop from a police family who had had to support some actions of her colleagues that she didn't really think were right. But she put her arm around me and gave me a brief hug. "I don't know how I could deal with a trigger-happy partner who killed someone and wanted to make me an accomplice. It must have been hell."

Chapter 7

KELAN SU

We strolled along the Grand Canal past a palazzo that was the former home of Peggy Guggenheim and now housed her brilliant modern art collection. Campari and I were fast becoming friends. I was extremely impressed with her pride in, and knowledge of, the cultural heritage of the city and her enthusiasm in describing it. To passersby, I thought we looked convincingly like a foreign visitors being shown the city by a friend who was a local.

As we neared Soledoro, I called Korb to report in as instructed. His response was "hmmph," which I took as approval. He was on his way to meet Strega at his apartment. The call ended with him curtly reminding me to report again in an hour.

The mask store was on a rio terra, a street laid out in cobblestones over a dry canal bed. When we reached the store, I was stunned. In front were two fantastic mannequins—one was outfitted with a black cloak, a black wide-brimmed hat, and a mask with a tremendous curved beak; the other, a harlequin, wore a bejeweled and enameled eye mask in amber and jade green. The store windows were a cornucopia of fantasies. There were gilded eye masks with feathers, sequins, and jewels; metallic face masks with enamel inlays grotesques with gargoyle features and serpentine hairdos; beaked portafortuna masks; white-faced Pierrots and Pierrettes with black teardrops. It was breathtaking. I was glad when Angela explained that the 13th-century *carnevale* tradition had been revived in the 1970s after being banned for almost 200 years and that the craft of mask-making had not only been preserved but improved upon.

We entered the store and began pointing at some of the most fabulous creations and exclaiming in amazement. The dour clerk's expression brightened as he sensed a sales opportunity. I asked about a particularly ornate mask. It was a moon-shaped, sad-eyed, white-faced woman with cupid's bow red lips, blue-shaded eyelids, and a blue tear on her left cheek. Her face was wrapped in a blue, star-studded scarf and encircled by bronze bows and ribbons. "Can you tell me about the symbolism and provenance of this mask?" I asked.

"An excellent choice," said the clerk with an approving nod. "This is one of the prize pieces of our master mask sculptor. It is a *bolla di natale* in the tradition of the 13th-century. It symbolizes aspects of the life of St. Francis of Assisi: his care for the natural world and his support of Clare of Assisi, often referred to as Sister Moon, and her Order of Poor Women. As a Christmas mask, the sad demeanor foreshadows the sadness of Mary, Christ's mother, and Mary Magdalene at the crucifixion. Our master sculptor has made only thirty numbered copies of this mask. You can see the number twenty-two on this one. Earlier ones have sold at over fifteen hundred euros, but I can offer you this one for eight hundred."

"I'll have to think about it," I said. The clerk's face resumed its sad expression, not unlike that of the mask, but without the tear.

Angela inquired, "Does the master sculptor work here? Could we see his workshop?"

"I am sorry, he is not here," said the clerk, glancing at the door. "He works in La Giudecca, an island in the southern part of the Dorsoduro. He is a recluse and does not allow anyone to view his work until we put it on display here. May I show you anything else?"

"You must have a large inventory of masks," I said. "Do you keep them all here? Are there other display rooms we may see?"

"This is our showroom. If you wish to see other masks, there is a computer display on that table with our entire catalog. Anything you might like to see, I will have an assistant fetch and bring it here. If you have no further questions, I must get back to my cataloging work. Have a nice day," he added dismissively. He turned back to his work behind the display counter.

Angela and I spent several more minutes in the showroom, ostensibly admiring the masks, but actually charting the room, its size, location in the building, entrances and exits. We chattered away about the masks, oohing and aahing at the creations. The clerk looked up occasionally scowling at us. After another five minutes, Angela and I left arm in arm and headed toward a café down the street with outdoor tables from which we could observe those who might enter or leave Soledoro.

We ordered coffee and luscious Venetian pastries. Angela chose two mini praline tarts, while I had a craving for chocolate. There were so many intriguing selections. The chocolate pastries seemed to have been influenced by the proximity of southern Germany. I opted for a thin, glazed, strudel dough pastry interlaced and filled with dark chocolate and sprinkled with pistachios. When our orders arrived, I realized it might be a problem not to let the sybaritic yumminess distract us from our main task.

Angela had a powerful Minox digital camera that looked like an MP3 player or, for the unredeemed, a cigarette lighter. In fact, she had brought a pack of cigarettes to complete the illusion, although she did not smoke. I was glad of that as I considered the number of smokers one of the few negatives of foreign travel.

Angela and I chattered gaily, sipped our coffee slowly, and munched contentedly on our pastries. We definitely looked happy, relaxed, and on holiday, though no one entering or exiting Soledoro escaped our notice. We also kept watch on a lower-level loading dock on the small canal at the rear of the store.

At first, only tourists were visiting the store—admiring, but not buying, just as we had done. Angela dutifully recorded them. As I was about to make my second call to Korb, a stick-thin, swarthy man walked swiftly by, entered the store, and almost immediately exited. He left with a round parcel wrapped in brown paper and tied with string. He briefly glanced up and down the street as if to check for someone watching. When he swung his head in our direction, Angela made to light her cigarette and snapped a photo. He hurried up the street in our direction. For a moment, I thought he had made us and would confront us. But he whisked past without looking our way.

I placed the call to my boss, reporting the substance of our encounters. I asked him what the procedure should be regarding suspicious characters entering and leaving the store. He offered no direct comment on our decision to stick by the store, simply muttering, "Use your own judgment." This was a rare expression of confidence, not easily recognizable to others. I asked him how his meeting with Strega had gone. His reply was a terse, "As good as could be expected." I didn't press for details, knowing that he hated to report to me, but would fill me in when he thought it absolutely necessary.

Maintaining our vigil, we ordered more coffee. It was getting late. I thought this was going to be a waste of time. The street began to fill with foot traffic, people returning home from work. Finally, we called for the check and were about to leave when a small cargo boat pulled up to the dock behind Soledoro. Two men unloaded several heavy-looking crates and carted them into the shop.

Angela and I looked at each other. Without a word, I slapped some euros down for the check and we headed to the store. The clerk was about to lock the door. We knocked and waved excitedly and shouted that we needed to speak to him. Reluctantly, he opened the door and said, "We are closed." His efforts to close the door again were thwarted by my foot and shoulder.

I said breathlessly, "Did you just get a new shipment of masks? Could we see them first? Was that the sculptor?" The clerk was taken aback as we pushed into the store. "Y-y-you can't be here. We're closed," he stammered.

"Ooooh, *per favore*!!!" Angela and I squealed in

unison.

"Those crates weren't masks. They were equipment. You have to leave now!" he said, regaining his composure.

"Mask-making equipment. Can we see how it works?" I asked.

"No, get out. I'll call the police."

"Go right ahead," said Angela, now looking serious.

The clerk blanched, sensing Angela's change of tone and realizing the foolishness of inviting the police into the store. "Now, I don't want to do that and you don't want to make trouble. Please go now and come back at eight-thirty tomorrow morning. The store doesn't open until nine, but I'll let you in to see any new things first."

Angela looked at me, widening her eyes questioningly. I sensed her question. Should she identify herself and ask questions in an official capacity? I shook my head almost imperceptibly. She read the signal. We headed for the door. I turned and said, "Tomorrow at eight-thirty. We'll expect something special."

After we left, the clerk hurriedly locked the door and drew the blinds but forgot to bring in the mannequins. Angela and I only barely stifled our laughter at his discomfiture. We walked away, glimpsing the boat as it pulled away from the dock. Angela took a picture of its retreating stern and partially obscured registration number.

Chapter 8

When Korb exited the hotel after speaking with Strega, Officer Treu was standing outside with a short, mustachioed man wearing a gray postman's uniform. The man, about fifty, had unnaturally black, shiny hair, deep-set dark eyes, and a long, narrow nose above his elaborately waxed and upturned mustache. Treu introduced the stranger as Silvio Martone, the Mayor of Cannaregio. "Mayor Martone," indicated Treu with a skeptical raising of his eyebrows, "has some interesting information."

Korb picked up on the slightly sarcastic tone of Treu's introduction of Martone as a mayor and his doubts about the value of his information. But the detective knew that the only way to get and evaluate the information was to humor the mayor. "I am very pleased to meet you, your Honor," said Korb with a slight bow. "I am sure there is no one who knows more about the goings-on in the sestiere than a mayor who is also a postman." Korb smiled.

"Thank you, Signor Korb. You won't be disappointed," said Martone. "I am also pleased to meet the renowned detective, Marko Korb. Your reputation precedes you." Martone returned Korb's bow, and they shook hands.

"What can you tell us?" said Korb, getting down to business.

The "mayor" took off his billed cap and wiped his brow with the sleeve of a somewhat tattered uniform. He took out a handkerchief and loudly blew his nose, carefully folding and returning the square of cloth to his pocket. He re-twirled his mustache ends. Martone took off his gold-rimmed glasses and squinted at them, checking for smears. He resettled the glasses on his nose. He knew how to build up the anticipation of his audience. "Well, you see," he began, "I was walking my beat on the night, or should we say, in the wee hours of the morning that Pakulić was murdered."

"Your beat?"

"Oh, yes. I am also a policeman and that night I had the midnight to eight shift," responded Martone with a prideful squaring of his shoulders. His hands again moved to preen his mustache. Treu rolled his eyes, which, fortunately, only Korb saw. This disdain earned Treu a hard glance from Korb.

"Please continue, sir," said the large man, moving slightly sideways to shift Martone's line of sight further from Treu.

"I shall, sir. As I was saying, I was patrolling in the Cannaregio during the midnight to eight shift. We call that the Deadly Night Shift because it seems that most violent crimes occur then." Martone paused for effect, again fingering his mustache. Korb managed to hold his show of impatience to a slight compression of the lips. Treu, looking extremely annoyed, barely suppressed a comment.

"Ah yes," said Korb, leaning forward in expectation.

"I was walking up Lista di Spagna on the morning of the murder," continued Martone, "when I heard a high-pitched scream—a woman's scream. As I tried to pinpoint the direction of the sound, I checked my watch. It was oh-two-thirty-eight hours. I then heard a shot and a second scream. This was followed by the clicking of a woman's high heels running on the cobblestone and another shot and then a splash. I tried to locate the source but saw no one. With the sound echoing off the buildings, I could not be sure which street was the locus," said Martone with an apologetic smile. "I rushed to the commissariat and arrived there at oh-two-fifty-five hours."

"And you reported this at the commissariat?" asked Korb, wondering why it had not been in the police dossier. Treu shook his head vigorously. The detective ignored him.

"Of course, I tried to, but the desk officer wouldn't take my report nor call the shift commander as I had requested," said Martone, his voice and grimace clearly showing shock and indignation. "He said, 'Martone, are you playing cops and robbers again? You know impersonating a police officer's a serious offense!'

"I told him that he was a fool and that the only one impersonating a police officer was he and doing a bad job at that!! Can you imagine? The imbecile threw me out!!" said "the Mayor" with a disgusted shake of his head. Again, he meddled with his mustache.

"Is there anything else you can remember about those early morning hours? Did you see anything that now strikes you as out of the ordinary?"

"Now that you ask, there was one thing." Martone's eyes focused somewhere in the distance. Korb questioned if Martone was trying to remember or fabricate an elaborate, self-aggrandizing lie. Was this story a product of a period of lucidity or the delusions of a madman?

"And what was that?" prompted Korb.

"There was a little dog running loose. It was barking frantically, dragging its leash. It was a sandy brown Corgi, I think. I had seen it before, being walked by a dark-haired, attractive young woman who, I believe, lives in the sestiere." A worried frown momentarily crossed Korb's features.

"Thank you, Signor Martone. Your report has been most helpful."

Martone nodded with satisfaction. Again, he twirled his mustache. The San Geremia bells rang out the hour. Martone frowned. "Signor Korb, I must be going. I have to convene a city council meeting to present my proposal for preventing the further sinking into the sea of my beloved Venice. It was a great pleasure to meet you and help you with your work."

"The feeling is mutual, your Honor, and best of luck to you in your many endeavors." They clasped hands in a strong, once up and once down European shake. The mayor, police officer, city engineer, postman, man of many hats did a military about-face and quick-stepped toward the nearby *vaporetto* stop.

As Korb and Treu watched, Martone stepped onto the crowded craft, took off his postman's hat, and deposited it in his bag, pulling out a naval officer's cap. Stepping to the prow of the boat, he placed the cap on his head, gave the *vaporetto* helmsman a crisp salute, and pointed dramatically down the canal.

Treu finally let the stifled hilarity rock through his body. "What a buffoon!!" he gasped between guffaws. "You know he has the full uniforms to go with the hats and he also has a major general's and a fire marshall's. You should have seen him at the big Castaleone fire. He was giving orders to all the fire crews and had to be restrained from charging into the building himself." Straightening up from his belly laughs and getting control of himself, he added seriously, "I'm sorry I let him bend your ear, sir."

Korb looked at Treu sternly. "If you ever expect to make Detective Inspector, Officer Treu, you will need to learn that it is not the quirks and peccadilloes of your informants that matter, it is their powers of observation and recollection. And they will part with their information more willingly if you treat them with respect. Signor Martone provided us with important information that the police had ignored. It included details not publicly available that made it credible. He is correct that he was the one acting professionally, not the desk officer who refused his report." Noticing Treu's chagrin, Korb added, "Perhaps a good cop's instinct prevailed, as you did bring him to me despite your personal lack of regard for him."

The lecture over, Korb indicated his desire to return immediately to the hotel. "It's getting late and I promised Chef Alberti that I would assist him in preparing the dinner tonight. You are welcome to join us. Inspector Mazzini, Detective Campari, and my associate will be there and will make their reports after dinner. Dinner will be at eight-thirty."

Chapter 9

Treu dropped his passenger off at the hotel dock after five, saying he would return for dinner at 8:30. When Korb entered the hotel, Su was talking to Chef Alberti. Alberti saw Korb first, stepped forward, and offered his hand. "*Buona sera,* Signor Korb. Are you ready to start the prep? Signorina Su has told me that we will have dinner for five at eight-thirty."

"Make it for six. You are, of course, invited," said Korb with a gracious incline of his head. "What are we serving?"

"We will start with *cicchetti*. That's a Venetian version of *tapas*, a selection of bite-size appetizers. We'll do a *salame di tonno*, *sarde in saor*, and *saliccia in balsamico*. *Il primo* will be a *risotto* with asparagus and *il secondo*, *capesante al basilico*. We will close with a cheese course and *granita di caffè con panna*, coffee ice with whipped cream followed by coffee and *limoncello*," recited Alberti, his round, red face glowing. "You may choose the wines from our cellar," he added.

"Superb!!" said Korb, a broad smile making his square-jowled bulldog face almost triangular. His mouth watered in expectation as he hurried off to change clothes–hurrying being something he only did in pursuit of a fine meal.

Korb changed into a high-collared, bone-white

shirt, a narrow, deep purple knit tie, white linen pants, and a charcoal, double-breasted, velvet blazer. He left on his charcoal socks and slipped his feet into charcoal canvas oxfords. Korb saved this "urban dandy" outfit for special occasions. Preparing a meal with Chef Alberti was a very special occasion. He only hoped there was a sufficiently large chef's apron to cover his ample, bedecked torso.

When the flashily dressed gourmet exited the creaky elevator in the hotel's wine cellar, Signor Giaccomo, the hotel proprietor, greeted him, clasping Korb's beefy hand in both of his. He was very proud of the well-stocked cellar. "Please help yourself to whatever you think will complement your meal." He added with an ingratiating smile, "And if you need any advice, I would be honored to consult with you."

"I have been told about your magnificent cellar, Signor Giaccomo," said the portly wine lover. "I am looking forward to browsing and making the selections. I will let you know if I have any questions." Korb hesitated. "Would you do me the honor of joining us for dinner tonight?" Giaccomo accepted gladly.

Korb walked down one of the three narrow aisles filled with rows of bottles of white wines. He relished the damp, musty air and was delighted with the additional four aisles of red wines. He was in his element.

He knew what he wanted for the *cicchetti*. It was a wine he always started important meals with. He was looking for a Prosecco Cartizze from Valdobbiadene, north of Venice. It was light, slightly sweet, semi-sparkling, and would go nicely with the tuna salami, sardine, and sausage dishes. Not the finest of wines, but it had a special significance for Korb. It was the last drink he had had with his sister, Sonja, and his friend, Sasha. A toast to the success of the mission that Korb was sending them on–the mission where they had met their deaths.

The bulky man took a little wheeled carriage the proprietor had indicated to him. It was a bit of a struggle on the cobblestone cellar floor and in the narrow aisles. Korb began to pull bottles of the Prosecco from the shelf to put in the carriage basket. As he pulled one bottle out, another one slid gently into place. He stared for a long moment at the newly ensconced bottle, raising one eyebrow and nodding his head.

The carriage bounced across the floor and the bottles clinked as Korb continued picking up the wines he had chosen for dinner—a Romano dal Forno Valpolicella for the risotto, a soave from Cantina del Castello for the basil scallops, a Slovenian Vipava Modri Pinot for the cheeses. This wine also had a connection to his narrow escape twenty-one years earlier, as it was the favorite among the fishermen who had taken him to Venice. The detective chose an Avignonese Vin Santo for the coffee and dessert. A satisfied smile flickered across the large man's bulldog face as he rattled and clanged his way back to the elevator.

When Korb left the elevator at the kitchen level, Chef Alberti and his two sous-chefs were hard at work. The excited gourmet showed Alberti the wines he had chosen for each course. Alberti smiled slightly and nodded his approval. He told one of his sous-chefs to ask Signor Giaccomo to prepare the wines for service.

The master chef wiped the sweat from his brow with a red kerchief as he asked, "Are you ready to work, Signor Korb? We don't have much time and you should be available to greet your guests."

"Yes, Maestro, if you have a large enough apron. Signorina Su can greet the guests. We are not having cocktails. What can I do?" said Korb, donning the huge apron handed to him by an assistant who helped the detective tie it off around his massive belly.

"We should probably start on the *cicchetti*. How are you at *aioli*? We need that for the tuna," said Alberti.

"One of my specialties," said Korb, beaming. "Do you have a food processor?"

"Of course, over on the corner counter. The eggs and lemons are already at room temperature. The garlic has been coarsely chopped. What kind of olive oil would you like?"

"Something from Tuscany–Lucca?"

"Georgio, get the Lucca for Signor Korb," ordered the chef.

For a moment, the detective's mind returned to childhood in his grandmother's rustic kitchen. She was making mayonnaise in a dented copper bowl. With an ancient whisk, the wrinkled, gnarly hands of the old woman creamed the fresh eggs he had fetched from the coop.

Korb put the chopped garlic in the food processor bowl. He cracked one of the eggs. Using the two halves of the shell, he separated the yolk from the white, discarding the white. He put the yolk into the processor bowl. He repeated the separation process with the other eggs. Then he added a teaspoon of salt. From the huge, wicker-covered olive oil carafe, mounted in a frame with a spindle, Korb poured out three cups of the viscous, gold-green substance which he set aside. He ran the machine in short bursts, beating the yolks until they had a creamy consistency. He began slowly pouring the oil, drop by drop, while running the processor. The mayonnaise began to thicken. Next, the expert amateur chef added a tablespoon of the fresh lemon juice a sous-chef had prepared and continued beating the mixture. He added more oil and lemon juice at a slightly faster rate. Finally, all of the oil and lemon juice had been absorbed and the mayonnaise looked lush and creamy. He handed it over to Giorgio who turned it into a serving bowl. With satisfaction, Korb could see the peaks raised by the spatula maintained their shape. He inhaled the deeply pungent aroma of the garlic.

Glancing over during the final stage of Korb's preparation, Alberti clacked his tongue approvingly and nodded. The head chef walked over to the huge stainless steel industrial fridge that let out a blast of cold air as he opened the door and walked inside. Emerging a moment later, he said, "The sweet and sour sardines are nicely marinated." Alberti handed the tray to an assistant for plating. "Signor Korb, can you start the sausage bites?" he asked. "The sausages have already been poached."

"*Certo*," said Korb, smiling almost gleefully. He added more of the Lucca oil to a skillet and turned on a burner of one of the two large gas stoves. He was handed the twelve house-made sweet sausages on a cutting board and began to slice them skillfully and rapidly into bite-size pieces. There was a muffled ratatat-tat as his professional levered slices severed the slightly firm links and made contact with the board. He brought the board to the skillet and swept the sausages into the now bubbling oil with the flat of the knife. The morsels gave a satisfying sizzle as the white-aproned cook stirred them with an ancient wooden spoon. They were soon a delicate brown, redolent of garlic, fennel, anise, oregano and mace. Korb's educated sense of smell could pick out each element of this savory bouquet. He closed his eyes tightly with a sonorous intake of breath.

A screened filter was placed at hand by one of the efficient, unobtrusive assistants. Korb lifted the skillet from the range and placed the filter over the sausages and poured off oil and fat into a metal container. He returned the pan to the stove, lowered the heat, and poured in two cups of the traditional balsamic vinegar of Reggio Emilia. This dark, *extra vecchio* decoction had been aged in cherry wood casks for 25 years. It gave off the rich, sweet, and pungent odors of the wood and the trebbiano grapes from which it was fermented. The dish simmered invitingly until the bubbling vinegar became thick and syrupy.

Alberti came to Korb's side. "Exquisite," he whispered as he, too, took in the aroma. "I and my assistants will finish up here. You must attend your guests."

Chapter 10

KELAN SU

Mazzini, Treu, and Campari arrived fashionably late, around 9:00. I tried to resist thinking *Italian time*. Fortunately, Korb was busy in the kitchen–one of the few places where he lost track of time. I greeted the guests and, with the help of Signor Giaccomo, made them comfortable in the dining salon. The innkeeper had seen to the service of the first wine Korb had chosen.

I was nervous. I wasn't the one they had come to see. Treu and Giaccomo were quiet, clearly feeling out of their element—Treu because he was outranked, Giaccomo because he was not part of the investigation. I made pleasant conversation, asking about families, the *Aida* production at the Fenice, and the center-left Italian government. When Angela told a funny story about her mother's new 50s-style rhinestone eyeglass frames, I raised my eyebrows and gave her a grateful look. I probably laughed too hard. *Dammit! Where was Korb?*

As Korb entered the dining salon, we all stared at his fanciful attire. He smiled blandly. I had only seen him once before in such a flamboyant outfit. Covering my surprise, I handed him a flute of the sparkling Prosecco. He nodded slightly. There were nervous murmurs of "*Buona Sera*" from the others.

"Good evening," Korb said. "I am happy to see that you are all here and that your glasses are filled with Signor Giaccomo's excellent Prosecco. Our *cicchetti* will arrive momentarily. We will owe much to his fine cellar and kitchen tonight." When Korb tried to be cordial, he usually sounded stiff and wordy.

A faraway look suddenly came over his face as he stared at his glass filled with the lightly golden, scintillating liquid. He raised the glass. "I would like to propose a toast," he said with a tight smile. "To fallen comrades." Hearing his grave tone, I closed my eyes. I knew what he meant.

With an involuntary shake of my head, I tried to rid myself of the melancholy feeling Korb's toast had engendered. I had thought of my brother and of Jerry Rodriguez, my best friend on the force, who had taken two bullets in the chest while making a routine traffic stop. He probably would have let the driver slide with a warning. When I heard the officer down call, I raced to the hospital and beat the ambulance to the emergency room only to see his eyes roll back and hear a last rasping rale as the EMTs slid him out. Jerry had been too sweet to be a cop. *Get off this, Su, or you'll be bawlin'!*

My lips formed a silent "*whew*" when the waiter brought in the *cicchetti*. It did look scrumptious. Korb brightened. "We have *salame di tonno* with *aioli*, *sarde in saor*, and *saliccia in balsamico*. Most of the credit goes to Chef Alberti and his efficient staff. I will take a little credit for the balsamic sausage bites and the *aioli*," he said, beaming proudly. "Please help yourselves." One waiter passed around small bone china plates, linen napkins, and cocktail forks while three other waiters, all in black, circulated with the dishes. I made sure the glasses were properly filled. There were admiring murmurs from the guests, both for the presentation and the first tastes. Korb was in his element.

Inspector Mazzini, between bites of sardine, asked almost lightheartedly, more to make conversation than to probe, "How did your first day of investigation go, Signor Korb?" Korb's brows furrowed deeply and his lips became a thin, tight, red line as his glare moved from Mazzini to me.

I blanched and coughed to hide my unease and collect my thoughts. *How to say it without ruffling feathers?* "I am so sorry," I stammered. "I should have told you all that Signor Korb never talks business during a meal. We will have time to discuss the case after coffee."

Several pairs of eyes widened in surprise or embarrassment. I quickly sat down in a brocaded wing chair and accepted a plate and helpings of the *cicchetti*. I took a long draught of the Prosecco and almost choked on it. Fortunately, no one noticed, as they were all pointedly directing their attention to their plates. Korb, of course, was oblivious to our discomfort. He sat down heavily in an overstuffed armchair, sipped his wine, rolling it on his tongue, and dug voraciously into his plate of hors d'oeuvres. Angela looked at me, shook her head slightly, and rolled her eyes sympathetically. Not for the first time, I was glad she had been assigned to this case.

The *cicchetti* course passed without further tension. The tastiness of the food and the mellowness of the Prosecco chilled out the assemblage. Me too, but getting tipsy was not in my job description. I asked about the revival of *carnevale* and the craft of mask-making. For a moment, Korb raised an eyebrow, listening for a possible slide into my part of the day's investigations. I kept the discussion light and general. Signor Giaccomo turned out to be very knowledgeable about the mask tradition. He smiled broadly, being able to contribute to the conversation, which he couldn't do if we talked about the case. Just as I was refusing a second glass of the sparkling wine, Chef Alberti appeared in the doorway to suggest that we take seats at the dining table in the next room.

Korb moved to the head of the table and I motioned Mazzini to his right and Alberti to his left. I sat at the foot with Angela on my right and Signor Giaccomo on my left. Treu took the remaining chair. Waiters ostentatiously poured the Romano dal Forno, an excellent valpolicella from Veneto. We all sniffed and sipped the dark ruby nectar. Eyes sparkled with pleasure. I could not contain my smile. The fragrance of sweet cherry and vanilla, underbrush, and spices wafted from the glass. My mouth marveled at the softness, harmony, and endurance of the fruity taste. My boss had gradually inducted me into the wine adorers' club. What a great accompaniment to the creamy, cheesy asparagus risotto the waiters had brought in and served. We sipped and ate, ate and sipped. The only sounds were the slight suctiony intake of the wine and the slurping, sticky chewing of the velvety risotto. We seemed to have lost the power to speak.

Korb finally broke the total concentration on taste and texture. Turning to Chef Alberti, he bowed his head with a slight nod and said, "My utmost compliments to the chef." This was followed immediately by "*si, si*" or "*bravissimo*" from the others. The chef inclined his head to one side and smiled, acknowledging the kudos. As the conversation resumed, I asked Alberti how he achieved the amazing consistency of the dish. "Ah," he said. "You must use more liquid than you would expect even after the rice is cooked. I combine a bit of cream with the stock, my secret ingredient, adding the stock until I get a somewhat wet mixture and then use the parmesan cheese to stiffen it a bit."

Much as I loved risotto, I didn't think I would try to make this dish myself. It seemed to require the instincts of a professional chef. Living with Korb and Des's fantastic meals has intimidated me. When I think of cooking, I tell myself, "Keep it simple, Su." I often retreat to the safe harbor of my mother's Chinese recipes.

The superb valpolicella was followed by an equally fine soave classico to accompany the basil scallops. By now, the conversation was flowing easily with a great deal of levity and also some heat. Italian politics are fascinating, if incomprehensible. I asked the company's opinions on the youthful Prime Minister Matteo Renzi. The lineup was interesting, but not what I'd expected. Giaccomo and Alberti, small businessmen with a long Venetian heritage, laughed heartily and approvingly when recalling how Renzi had engineered the takeover of the Democratic Party and condescendingly dismissed the old way of doing party business. They would not normally support left-center politicians. Mazzini and Campari, public servants with family in the south, were ticked off by Renzi's arrogance and by the fact that he was playing ball with Berlusconi's parliamentary troops. But they also recognized that the PM needed the rightist votes in the Senate for the electoral reforms he was pushing. Treu was mostly silent, contributing a few gruff *si*s. I suspected he was hard-core left, possibly a Communist.

The wine and superb food began to get to me too. I started to relax–maybe too much, beginning to feel some numbness in my fingertips. I found myself wanting to laugh at comments whose humor escaped me.

Through the cheese course with the light and velvety Slovenian Vipava Modri Pinot, the conversation waned. I felt the lethargy, which a bellyful of succulent food and several glasses of fine wine brings to any normal human. My eyes were closing. I looked around me and noticed the other guests were also mellowed out and near slumber. They were leaning back in their chairs with their heads at various relaxed angles, eyelids drooping, appearing to be contemplating inwardly the pleasures that the sense of taste can bring.

All except Korb. Although he had drunk and eaten more than the rest of us, he was observant. His eyes moved from one guest to another, taking in the state of their alertness. He seemed satisfied. I could not imagine why if he expected to discuss the case later. Our host indicated to a waiter to bring in the dessert, a coffee ice with whipped cream, accompanied by a vin santo. *Caffeine and sugar to begin the waking process?*

"Let's take coffee in my sitting room," said the huge detective, rising with surprising ease. I found it difficult to get up from the table. With a firm grip on the arms of my chair, I pushed up. I almost couldn't feel my feet. Once up, I felt better. "*Let me at a triple espresso,*" I thought.

The other diners rose slowly, accompanying their ascent with stifled groans and steadying hands on the table or chair arms. As we noticed our own groping and somnolent appearance, grimaces changed to sheepish half smiles. After that quick exchange of glances, we all lowered our eyes to the floor as much for balance as to cover up our embarrassment. *What a suave, cosmopolitan crew!!*

Korb led us to the small elevator. The door slid open slowly. He opened the gate and squeezed in. The elevator creaked and shuddered with his weight. There wasn't much room left. Inspector Mazzini bravely stepped in. The rest of us exchanged questioning looks. Chef Alberti immediately excused himself, saying, "I must supervise the kitchen clean up and prep for tomorrow's meals. Thank you for including me as a dinner guest. I rarely get the chance to sit down and fully enjoy my own cooking."

Korb nodded, smiling to acknowledge his gratitude to the chef. Seeming to have regained his equilibrium, Alberti smartly turned on his heel and left the group. Signor Giaccomo also excused himself, as he was not to take part in the investigation's discussion. He thanked the detective profusely for including him in this *"magnifico"* culinary experience. Our host thanked him for lending the facilities of his hotel for "my little dinner party."

Discretion being the better part of valor, Campari, Treu, and I said we would take the stairs rather than use the heavily loaded elevator. The exercise might clear my head and get my joints, stiff from sitting, working again. I led the way to the second-floor sitting room. On the way up, Angela asked if the case discussion would start over coffee or only after. "After," I said, "if the caffeine keeps us from falling asleep." She chuckled, but Officer Treu frowned as if trying to reestablish his powers of concentration.

Mazzini and Korb had not yet arrived on the floor when we entered the hall. It took several more seconds before the pokey elevator stopped uncertainly on the second floor. As he and my bulky boss exited, gingerly stepping up the two-inch rise caused by the lift's inaccurate stop, the Inspector mumbled something about "an exciting ride." I was glad I had taken the stairs.

The sitting room was lined with bookcases and leather-bound books. The sofas and armchairs were upholstered in supple, well-worn cordovan leather. The room smelled of lemony furniture polish and the sweet, slightly musty odor of the fine old leather—aromas of elegance that set off the earthy, pungent smell of the espresso and coffee granita. The small glasses filled with limoncello increased the smell of lemon.

Korb marched directly to the gargantuan, heavily cushioned armchair that dominated the room and sat down heavily. He motioned the rest of us to take our seats. Angela and I plopped down on the sofa that was at Korb's right. Mazzini and Treu took armchairs facing Korb.

We all looked at the detective expectantly. "First we eat," our host warned with a slight smile. The light dessert slid down agreeably despite all that I had eaten. Its coolness helped to revive me a bit. I noticed that all but Korb skipped the vin santo and opted for the coffee. The limoncello remained untasted.

Chapter 11

KELAN SU

Korb took a long sip of coffee and closed his eyes momentarily. He patted his lips daintily with his napkin. Looking at each of his guests, he said, "Well, I hope you enjoyed our little repast."

"*Molto grazie,* Signor Korb," said Angela, half-smiling at his understatement. "The food and the wines were exquisite." The others all nodded enthusiastically. "I hope our reports are sufficient recompense for this extravaganza," she added. I loved how my partner was not put off or cowed by Korb's eccentricity.

"Ahh, yes," exhaled Korb, bobbing his head and returning Angela's half-smile. "The reports. It's time we get to those." The hefty detective shifted in his chair and looked at me, raising one eyebrow. "Ms. Su, will you begin?"

I nodded and rose from my seat. Collecting my thoughts, I glanced at Angela, who nodded her complicity. I don't know why reporting made me nervous. I had reported to parents, teachers, bosses, judges, and colleagues all my life. But each time, I had butterflies, sweaty palms, and a dry mouth. Taking a deep breath and licking my lips slightly, I recounted how we had staked out and entered Soledoro that afternoon. After I had covered the skinny man and boat we saw, Angela chimed in about snapping the pictures. Korb suggested that Angela continue the report. I gratefully ceded the floor to her, sitting back a bit heavily with a sigh of relief.

I envied Angela's aplomb. She didn't stand. She merely moved to the edge of her seat and leaned forward, looking hard at Korb. My boss glared back momentarily but then seemed to relax, leaning back in his chair and steepling his hands under his chin. His eyes widened with interest as Angela began her report. *You go, girl!* I thought.

Angela elaborated on my description of the shop and the clerk. She had a good ear for local accents and a great memory. Her take on the clerk's height, weight, and coloring tallied perfectly with mine. She noted a slight scar on his eyebrow, which I had missed. She had pegged his accent to southern Italy, most likely Naples. The only thing she missed was the slightly pointy shape of his ears. I always check ears as they're often distinctive identifiers. We agreed on the appearance of the man who had exited the shop with the package.

When Angela said she had run the pictures through the identification databases, I sat up straighter. As we thought, most of those who entered the store were absent from the databases, most likely tourists. Only three photos turned out to be significant. The clerk had a criminal record, including prison time for burglary and theft. The rail-thin, swarthy man who exited with a package was Tiziano Massimo, the neo-fascist enforcer.

The third picture was of a small, dark woman, about sixty years old, in a brown pants suit, who entered the store but did not exit during our time in the area. She held a low-level Serbian diplomatic post during the Bosnian War, but was suspected of being the handler of a major spy network. She had worked under Aleksandr Vucic, who was now the Serbian Prime Minister. Her name was Paola Chekova.

The shot of the partial registration number of the boat unloading crates turned up another interesting detail. It was a lighter registered to the Greek cargo ship Parthenon, owned by Agamemnon Constantinides. The shipping magnate was a major supporter of Rising Sun, a Greek neo-fascist movement. The shipping company, under his father, had been an important bankroller of the Greek military junta, finally ousted in 1974. Of course, with their millions, the company and the family had no trouble surviving the junta's demise. Agamemnon continued to fund neo-fascist parties. The company was rumored to be a major supplier of weapons to these movements.

Angela paused and took a deep breath.

Korb said, "Do you have anything to add?"

"I do," she said, "but it's highly speculative."

"Proceed," said Korb, leaning forward. "I am interested in hearing your notions."

Whew!! Did Angela know that this was like winning a Nobel prize?

She looked around the room. Four pairs of eyes were riveted on her. "It occurred to me," she began, "that June 28 of this year is the 100th anniversary of the 1914 assassination of Archduke Franz Ferdinand by Gavril Princip. The killing took place in Sarajevo, Bosnia. Princip is considered a Serbian hero who saw Bosnia as Serbian national territory. That date would be a draw for a major terrorist action against Bosnians. Serbia has never signed a peace treaty with Bosnia.

Pakulić was supposed to be in Italy to arrange some kind of action. Rumor has it that he was given a tidy sum to arrange it and failed to deliver. He spent the money on his vices–vodka, prostitutes, gambling. If so, both the Serbian and Italian neo-fascists had a strong motive to get rid of him.

There was an appreciative silence. Each guest had a pensive look pondering Angela's conjecture. *Another point for Angela in my book.* Only Korb seemed skeptical. He looked hard at Angela and said, "The evidence you have recounted does not support this speculation. Do you have anything more?" *Typical Marko Korb.*

"I don't," she said but didn't seem discouraged. *Good for her.* The genius detective never credited anybody's theories but his own. *Right on! Another good reason to leave this investigation to the police.*

I hesitated, but I wanted to support Angela. "I like it," I said. My chief's eyes narrowed as he looked at me. I held his gaze. "Maybe we can turn up something when we go back to Soledoro in the morning." Korb pursed his lips and closed his eyes, leaning his head against the chair-back. *Was I fired?*

Mazzini cleared his throat, attracting the group's attention. He nodded at Angela and me. He began slowly. "Signor Korb, I know that you have a low opinion of the acumen of the police. But we do have our sources. One is an informant inside Golden Dawn. There's definitely something brewing with right-wing Serbians. The Bosnian community here is the obvious target. Pakulić was involved. He was in Greece too. Weapons are being stockpiled, and we need to find them. It seems that Detective Campari and Ms. Su are on the right track." *Inspector Mazzini to the rescue. Thank you!!*

Korb steepled his fingertips, leaned forward, and glared over them at the Inspector. "It seems there is a trend of opinion that Pakulić's death was related to his involvement in a neo-fascist conspiracy. Possibly Officer Treu's report on our encounter with Silvio Martone will raise some doubts about that theory." The leader of this discussion nodded at Treu, who huffed nervously.

The officer narrated the fantastical encounter with "Mayor" Martone and his story about the running young woman. A suppressed chuckle escaped my lips, but Treu, noting my skepticism, added that he, too, had supposed Martone to be a crackpot and his story a fanciful attention grab. When he had checked out the refusal to accept the report by the desk officer, he was surprised to hear that Martone's reports were not inaccurate. He was seen as a nuisance because he had reported many incidents that were considered too trivial to expend police time. The informal policy was to ignore him. Mazzini looked downcast at this. We had police groupies like that in Chicago. We adopted the same attitude. Leave it to Korb to see the value in extracting this information.

"Could Martone ID the woman?" Mazzini asked.

Treu frowned and shook his head. "Still working on that, Inspector," he replied.

Something in Korb's expression at that moment made me think he knew more about this than he was saying. I looked at him questioningly, and he avoided my glance. He quickly said, "Well, these reports have given us a lot to ponder and we have a heavy schedule tomorrow. Kelan, you and Detective Campari will return to Soledoro."

I looked at Angela, nodded, and said, "Check, Boss," earning me a disapproving look. I was so tired I didn't care at this point if Korb fired me on the spot. At least I'd be able to sleep late.

Our leader continued, "Officer Treu and I will return to the Cannaregio to interview others in the Bosnian community and the neighborhood of the crime scene. Inspector Mazzini, I would appreciate it if you would plumb your informants for more on Pakulić's activities since he has been in Venice. Tomorrow night Ms. Su and I will take in the casino. Thank you all for your help. Please feel free to contact me if you have anything to add. I bid you a good night." Korb heaved himself out of his chair, glanced around with slight nods to each of us, and left the room.

I was used to his abrupt exits. The others were caught off-guard at being so summarily dismissed. They were looking from one to the other with puzzled expressions. I stood up, feeling a bit woozy. "Thank you for everything you are doing and for your tolerance of my boss's lack of social graces. Despite appearances, your work is greatly appreciated. Has everyone arrangements to get back home?" They all indicated they were okay.

Then back to business. "Angela, we'll pick you up at eight a.m. tomorrow. Not much sleep, I'm afraid. Officer Treu, will you be able to be back here at seven-thirty?" Treu rolled his eyes as he agreed. *What an evening! I hope I can get to my room before I crash.*

Chapter 12

The next morning, Korb and Treu pulled up again at Strega's hotel. Korb hated being up and about this early in the morning. Treu leapt onto the dock and tied up the launch. With Treu's assistance and several guttural grunts, the stout detective managed to climb out of the boat and onto the dock. Two more chuffs and Korb made the three steps to street level. He took two deep breaths, pulled a large white silk handkerchief from his pocket, and mopped his brow. The huge dinner, several bottles of wine, and the late night had taken its toll. Not that Korb could ever be called spry. Turning to the officer, he handed over a folded sheet of paper. Treu's brow furrowed as he perused the note.

"That is a list of employees and long-term guests at the Albergo. While I am with Signor Strega's daughter, talk to as many of them as you can. Find out where they were shortly before, during, and after the murder. What did they see at the time and what did they hear then and since? Ask them about each other's whereabouts."

Treu cupped his chin and lips with one hand as his eyes narrowed in thought. He nodded his understanding to Korb.

"We'll meet back here in two hours. Right?"

"*Certo.*"

Korb watched Treu enter the hotel, then turned away. Giving his cane a Chaplinesque twirl, he strode

down the street. At a small café, he stopped and looked
into the dimly lit interior. Making his way past side-
stepping waiters, he headed toward a small table in the
darkest corner of the room. He wedged his ample
derriere into a banquette against the wall that faced the
door. He placed his hat and cane on the table and
proceeded to signal a young man wearing a white shirt,
black pants, and a white apron.

The waiter approached the table, looked down at
Korb, and said, "Signor?"

Korb looked up and said, "*Espresso doppio, per
favore.*"

Acknowledging the order with a nod, the waiter
turned toward the bar, stopping to sweep some coins off
a nearby table. With a look of distaste, Korb wiped the
spillage off the table with his handkerchief. After some
squirming and a grunt, the portly detective extracted an
ornate pocket watch, opened the gilt cover, glanced at
the time, and grimaced.

The waiter returned with the coffee, setting it
down. "*Qualcos'altro,* Signor?"

Korb shook his head and dismissed the waiter with
a slight wave of his hand. Looking at the coffee, he
contemplated the froth on the surface. He breathed in
deeply the rich, toasty aroma of the brew and slowly
lifted the steaming liquid to his lips.

After that first sip, Korb raised his head and looked
toward the door. Silhouetted in the doorway was a
young woman with long, dark hair. She peered inside,
her eyes unadjusted to the gloom. Finally, she spotted
Korb in his shadowy corner. Hesitating slightly and
then straightening to her full height, she entered the
café. Feigning an air of confidence, Strega's daughter

strode toward the table. With a flick of his head, the proprietor behind the bar signaled to some customers that they ought to take a look at what had just come in. Appreciative smiles and nods were exchanged by the men turning from their morning espressos or grappa to watch the voluptuous young woman.

Even Korb was momentarily stunned by this brunette beauty moving with a graceful sway toward him. Mia Strega stopped before Korb's table. Her long lashes lowered slightly over her striking green eyes as she asked, "Signor Korb?" The large man made to rise. Noticing his outstanding bulk, Strega waved her hand for him to stay seated and quickly settled herself into the chair opposite.

"Signorina Strega, so good of you to come," said Korb. The waiter appeared at the table looking a question at the girl. Korb raised his hand palm up, motioning toward her. She shook her head.

"The note you left with my father seemed like a summons," she said with a tight smile. "Did I have a choice?"

"You know why I'm here, Signorina," said Korb with a piercing look.

She met his eyes for an instant and then lowered them as she breathed, "Yes."

"Tell me about the night of the killing, starting from the time you got home from work."

Strega nodded slightly, hesitated, and began, "Well, I arrived home between six and seven. My father and I had dinner together and watched some television." Her eyes suddenly shifted to Korb's left and then down to the table. When she looked up again, she continued, " I was very tired. Around midnight, I usually walk the dog before going to bed, but my father said he would do it. So I went to sleep."

"And did you sleep soundly?" said Korb, exhaling and raising his eyebrows.

Strega frowned. "Yes," she said, a bit too strongly.

"So you don't know when or if your father went out to walk the dog?"

"No. But if he hadn't taken him out, there would have been crazed barking and a stinking mess in the morning," was her flip answer. Strega gave her interrogator a wry smile. Korb's lips puckered and his eyes narrowed. He didn't like her attitude.

"Miss Strega, the police have a witness who heard a woman running away after a shot was fired and saw a small dog running loose away from the scene. His description of the dog matches that of your dog," Korb said with a stern look. "Your father's covering for you is not going to work except to incriminate him. Level with me, missy, and I might be able to help."

Strega looked up at Korb, and then down to her hands folded on the table. She did not reply. The detective took his hat and cane and pried himself out of the seat. Strega's head was still down, but now her eyes were shut tight. The large man frowned and shook his head almost imperceptibly. For a moment, he looked infinitely sad. "You have my number," he said as he glanced down at her hunched shoulders. Korb tapped his cane twice and waddled to the door.

Chapter 13

After leaving the café, Korb stopped for a moment and pulled out his pocket watch. The detective flipped open the cover and checked the hour. He had some time to kill before meeting up with Treu. It was too early for lunch. Frowning, the large man looked around, not sure what he would do next. The conversation with Mia Strega was disappointing. Korb knew that both she and her father were lying. Both had strong motives for hating Pakulić. Rumor had it that the death of Strega's wife, the girl's mother, had been under torture by Pakulić's henchmen. As with most Bosnians, they had surely lost friends and relatives to Serbian barbarism.

Although Korb detested walking, he retraced the route from the albergo to the crime scene, hoping that might stimulate his brain cells. His cane striking rhythmically with each step, he ambled along the Lista di Spagna in the direction of the hotel. Squinting in the sunlight, his keen eyes drank in the surroundings: the lapping canal waters and docks on his right; shops, two cafés, and a small hotel on his left. The shops were busy, particularly the bakeries and a greengrocer. The cafés were now empty, with aproned waiters preparing tables for the lunch crowd. The hotel looked seedy and forlorn, lacking the slightly frayed elegance of Strega's Albergo Ponte e Palazzo.

Korb noted a portly, middle-aged man entering the

hotel arm-in-arm with a mini-skirted, much younger woman. The woman was a pale-skinned, peroxide blonde, who wore bright red lipstick, dangling earrings, and a Marilyn Monroe pout. The man kept his head down with a fedora pulled low to shade his jowly face. He whispered something in his companion's ear. A heavy sadness came upon Korb. The Lista di Spagna was replete with hotels where rooms could be rented by the hour, and in this neighborhood, with young Bosnian girls who had no means of support other than selling their bodies.

With a slight frisson, Korb pushed aside the depressing thought as he entered the Campo San Geremia. At the opposite end of the Campo was a bridge leading to the Rio Terra San Leonardo, the heart of the crime scene. The rio went to the rear of the Palazzo Vendramin-Calera. It was at the campo end of the bridge that Pakulić was most likely shot and fell into the Cannaregio Canal. Korb halted at the bridge. He made a half-turn to his left and looked up the Canal. Both sides were lined with three and four-story buildings. There were storefronts on the canal level and apartments above. Then, turning to his right, he saw the Palazzo Labia, which contained administrative offices, priests' quarters, and an elementary school for the adjoining San Geremia church.

Korb closed his eyes, lifted his head, and sniffed the air. As he opened his eyes, his arm and cane seemed to be rising of its own accord, directed by a playful spirit. He found the cane was pointing to an overhang at the angle made by the Palazzo Labia and San Geremia. He lowered the cane and walked toward the overhang as if in a trance. When he reached the spot, he realized why he had been drawn there. Passing by earlier, he had seen something, not consciously noted, that must have been filed at the back of his mind. On the cobblestone pavement under the overhang were several flattened cardboard boxes. Korb stared at them for a moment and tilted his head, squinting into the distance. Giving a sharp rap to the pavement with his cane, he turned toward the entrance of the church.

San Geremia was not a tourist attraction. It was a working-class church, more than a bit rundown–peeling and chipping paint, worn and gouged pews, terrazzo tiles missing, even a statue of the Virgin Mary missing her nose. When Korb entered, the church was silent and empty except for three black-shawled old women with heads bowed in the second row of pews. In a dimly lit apse to Korb's right, a sexton was placing new candles in a wooden receptacle. Korb approached the man. "*Signor, un attimo per favore.*"

The man looked up from his work. "*Si?*"

"I saw some large cardboard boxes flattened in the piazza."

"Oh, yeah. Haven't gotten to them yet. Is it a problem?" said the sexton, his brow furrowing.

"I'd like to know what you do with them."

"I just stack them in a shed until nighttime."

"Until nighttime? And then?" queried Korb, curious, but impatient.

"Then I put them back in the piazza."

"Yes, but why?"

"This is a very poor sestiere," said the sexton. "There are many poor devils with no place to sleep. Some of them come here. We have sleeping bags and, for privacy, the boxes. If the weather is very bad, we let them sleep in here on the pews."

"Are there people sleeping here every night?" asked Korb.

"Yes."

"Is it usually the same people who come?"

"It varies. We do have regulars who have been coming here for years."

"I would like to talk with them tonight. Would it be all right if I and my colleague come by? What time do most of the people arrive?"

"Why do you need to know this?" said the sexton, his eyes narrowing.

"It is very important that I ask them a few questions."

"Sir, this is not a talkative bunch. They fear strangers. Especially those who ask questions. We don't like to intrude upon their privacy, little as it is," said the sexton, massaging his forehead with his fingertips. "I'll have to ask Father Ignacio, our Rector."

"Is Father Ignacio here? I will be happy to ask him myself and explain the reasons."

"Wait here. I'll get him."

Korb nodded and sat in the nearest pew, emitting a sigh as he took a load off his feet.

Father Ignacio was an ugly, short, swarthy man with a bulbous nose and bowed legs, giving him a rolling sailor's gait. Despite his comical appearance, he had an unquestionable air of dignity. His deep-set dark eyes shone with intelligence and compassion. He extended his hand immediately and shook Korb's hand firmly. "I understand you wish to talk to the unfortunates who sleep in our piazza," said the priest.

"Yes, Father. If I might explain." The priest

nodded.

Korb explained who he was and why he wanted to speak to the homeless folks.

Father Ignacio pursed his lips and blew out his cheeks, hesitating before answering. "I believe that is possible. Come back tomorrow night so I might have a chance to talk to the people and be sure they are willing."

"Father, I would very much prefer that you do not tell them and that I might speak with them tonight. I don't want them to disappear or to rehearse responses. I promise not to use any form of coercion on them. If they do not wish to speak with me, I will not press them."

Ignacio exhaled, bowed his head, and pressed his fingers to his forehead. "Very well, Signor Korb. I will only tell them when you arrive that they should hear you out but need not answer your questions. I know your reputation and I will trust you not to put these people in jeopardy."

Korb reassured the priest that he and his associate would be the souls of discretion.

Chapter 14

KELAN SU

We arrived at Soledoro at 8:00 a.m., half an hour before our appointment at the store. Angela and I ensconced ourselves at the same café we had found the day before and ordered coffee. Food was out of the question after last night. I sighed as I sipped the double espresso. The rich aroma helped to wake me up after a sybaritic evening and a fitful sleep. We talked about how we should proceed. Frankly, I had no clue. Korb had given no instructions.

"Let's continue playing tourists," suggested Angela.

"Keep asking questions and see what pops up?"

Angela nodded.

"The clerk just showed up. Let's go," I said, jumping to my feet. We blathered gaily and linked arms on the way to the shop. As we reached the door, the clerk was just coming out, dragging one of the mannequins, this time a Pierrot in a white mask and satin clown costume. A Pierrette, similarly attired, was just inside the door. When he saw us, his eyes opened wide and an "uhh" came from his gaping mouth. He nearly dropped the mannequin. I smiled pleasantly and said, "*Buongiorno,* Signor. Remember us?"

"*Si, si, si,*" said the clerk quickly, the corners of his

mouth turning down abruptly.

"We've come back for the special showing you promised us." I gave him a knowing half smile, hoping it would add to his unease. "You said you'd show us some new things."

Hesitating for a moment, the clerk said, "Yes, we did receive a shipment last night. Not from our master mask maker, but from another master. Franco specializes in devil masks. He is also Venetian. All of the masters are."

He brought out the Pierrette figure and then locked the door behind him on reentering. "So we won't be bothered by other customers," he said.

I raised my eyebrows to Angela, who inclined her head and patted her purse where she carried her service weapon. "Let's see those masks," I said. "Is Franco one of your regular suppliers?"

"Yes."

Angela chimed in with, "Where is his shop located? We would love to see a master in action."

The clerk ignored Angela's question as he brought out a large tray, on which were six devil masks. The leering, red-lipped smile and hooded eye sockets made my stomach churn. Although the shape, triangular and narrow with curving horns, was the same for all, each mask had a different surface color and texture. One was shiny obsidian, another antique gold. There was a mottled white, an iridescent emerald green, a scarlet, and a turquoise blue. The clerk smiled as he noted our startled reactions.

The masks were spectacular, but I couldn't have the clerk feel like he was gaining the upper hand. I had done my research. "I heard that Lovati was the real master of devil masks. Do you have any of his?"

The clerk frowned. "Lovati is tied to Ca' Magano. They do not deal with us."

The buzzer went off in my head. "Professional rivalry or artistic differences?"

The clerk shook his head quickly, eyes widening in surprise.

"Could it be political differences?" I said, giving the clerk a knowing smile. He swallowed hard.

"What do you mean, Signorina?" he said, frowning.

"Oh, nothing *really*," I said, hoping my tone would imply forbidden knowledge.

"Are you interested in buying a mask or not?"

I wanted to see more of their operation. "We would certainly consider buying masks if we could see some being made by a master," I said, emphasizing the plural. "Can't you set up an appointment so we can watch one of your masters in action?"

"No, I cannot." He removed the tray of devil masks from the counter. "I am sorry. I must open the store now." He stepped to the door, unlocked it, and flipped the hanging sign to *Aperto*.

As he turned back to remove the tray of masks, Angela said, "Mr. Constantinides told us that your master is a genius." This got a definite rise from the clerk. His head snapped up and he nearly dropped the display tray.

"Who did you say?" he quickly said.

"Mr. Constantinides, Agamemnon was his first name, I think. We met him in Athens. He was very charming and knowledgeable about your operation here," she added. "He said that your masks were exquisite and we would be supporting a good cause if we patronized your store. He asked us to be sure and email him with pictures of any masks we bought."

"And he said to give you this message. 'The eye of the storm has passed, but the winds will rise again.' What was that all about?" I asked.

The clerk shook his head as if to clear a mental fog. He started to breathe rapidly. For a moment, I thought he might be having a heart attack. "Please, you must go now," he said, ushering us toward the door. "Tell Mr. Constantinides that you have delivered the message and it was understood." He unlocked the door, almost shoved us out, and quickly locked the door behind us. He flipped the sign again. It swung from side to side, reading *Chiuso* to the outside world.

Several tourists who had been heading for the shop balked in amazement. "Well I never," said a heavy-set, sensibly shod English lady as she plowed into one of her companions who had stopped short in front of her. "These Italians are really too much," She stooped to help the woman who had been knocked to the ground.

Outside, eyes wide in amazement, Angela spluttered, "Where did you get that 'eye of the storm' thing? I thought he was going to faint."

"Well, it certainly got the pot boiling," I said with a broad grin.

Chapter 15

KELAN SU

"Either someone will leave or someone will come now," said Angela. "Where should we watch from?"

"They'll spot us at our usual café table," I said. "There's a food cart just below the foot of the bridge there. We can see arrivals by foot or canal as well as departures and we'll be blocked from view." I added ruefully, "A food cart! I swear I'll gain ten pounds on these stakeouts. Just being near that wonderful Venetian street food makes me hungry."

Angela nodded her assent, and we headed across the cobblestone bridge. The sun reflected brightly off the water, almost blinding me. I pulled some Ray-Ban eyeglasses from my purse and put them on. The glare subsided. My breath caught at the beauty of the scene– rippling water gently lapping the stone piers; cerulean sky with a few puffy, white clouds; delicately arched stone bridge with carved masonry; colorful awnings and umbrellas lining the banks of the canal. I had to shake myself loose from this reverie. It's too easy to forget my work here.

"Angela, if the clerk leaves, you tail him. He'd spot me sooner. Anyone else comes out is mine. Keep in touch by cell if we separate."

"Right."

We didn't have long to wait. The clerk came out at a run from the lower canal level of the store. He burned right past us as we ducked behind the red and green umbrella of the food cart. Angela raised an eyebrow and tapped herself on the chest. She took off at a trot after the clerk. Good stride. She must be a runner. I thought of all the workouts I had missed since coming to Venice.

I decided to walk past the store to see if anything was going on. From my vantage point at the foot of the bridge, I couldn't see any activity. I didn't think anyone else at the store had spotted me. I paid the cart man for a pineapple gelato cone. As I headed down the canal toward the store's loading dock, I took a big lick. Wow! I knew Italian ice cream was the best, but this creamy, sweet, but slightly tart concoction was heavenly. I almost stumbled as I savored my second lick. The cop in me urged restraint. If I didn't eat the gelato too fast, I could use it to hide my face if I spotted anyone who could ID me.

The loading dock entrance to the store was covered by a corrugated metal garage door. The folding metal gate that would have barred the entrance was not closed. Either there was still someone in the store or the clerk, in his haste, had been careless. There was one barred window above the metal door at the showroom level. I didn't see any lights or movement. Backtracking to the foot of the bridge, I went up to the front entrance of the store. I made like a curious window shopper, moving close to the glass while keeping my cone in front of my face. No lights, no movement. I knocked on the door to see if anyone would respond. Nothing. I tried the knob. Locked.

Maybe foolish, but I couldn't resist. I retraced my steps to the dock entrance while quickly finishing the cone. "Mmmm." At the metal door, I listened for a long moment. No sound. I squatted at the bottom of the door and squeezed my hand under and lifted slowly and carefully. Metal slats and rollers would not be silent. If anyone were there, my goose was cooked. I removed my sunglasses and turned my cell phone ringer off.

I lifted the door just enough to duck under and carefully slid it back down to the ground. With my eyes unadjusted to the dark, I saw nothing. I waited. No lights, no voices, no muzzle flashes. I guess I was lucky. I took a small LED flashlight from my purse and panned it around the room, aiming it close to the floor to avoid windows. Pallets of crates were stacked along two sides of the room. At the rear was a freight elevator and a stairway to the upper floor, and to the right of the stairway was what looked like an office.

I wanted to examine those crates and their contents. They were labeled with Greek writing. With my limited knowledge of the language of Socrates, I could just make out "Constantinides Shipping." *Beware of Greeks bearing gifts.* One stack was only two crates high. Leaning against one of the pallets was a crowbar. *How convenient!* I partially pried open one of the lids, being careful not to damage the crate and leave a trace of my presence. I reached in and felt straw with something underneath encased in bubble wrap. Moving the straw and shining my flash in, I saw that the wrapped items were unpainted and unadorned mask forms. *Hmmm. Weren't Soledoro's mask makers local? Why are they getting mask forms from Greece?*

I took out a mask and examined it. It seemed to be

made of a partially hardened putty. Unlike the feel of the masks I had seen earlier. Possibly some kind of baking or glazing process would be used after the mask was decorated. The putty had an acrid, tar-like odor, with a touch of sweetness. I had smelled that aroma before. *But where?*

I rewrapped the mask and slid it back into the crate. Then it hit me. *Sheeeeit! C4!!!.* The smell was from a hexanol derivative used in making the plastic explosive. I had found this stuff in the crib of a gangbanger in Chicago. I carefully replaced the lid of the crate. Looking around at the stacked crates, I tried to estimate the firepower in that room. *Christ! Enough to return the entire city of Venice to the sea. What the fuck were these assholes planning?*

I should get out of here and warn the cops ASAP. But it sure would be nice to have a chain of documents putting this together and tying in the participants. Whoa there, Su. Let's not get greedy. Yeah right. Pass up a chance to check out the office. No way!

I shifted my flash to the office door. Cheap wood with a glass window. I could easily break in, but wanted to avoid setting off any alarms or leave a trace of my entry. The door opened into the loading area with the curved handle on the left. A standard pin tumbler lock was visible and, as I looked down through the window, I saw a curved handle with a push button lock. *No sweat. These people were either stupid or incredibly confident–probably both—one often led to the other.*

Holding the flashlight in my mouth, I took out my picks. Sticking the right-angled tension wrench into the bottom of the lock, I applied torque–first clockwise and then counterclockwise. There seemed to be more give in the clockwise direction. I kept the tension in that direction light and inserted the curved tip of the pick into the lock point up above the wrench. I raked the tip across the pins, trying to feel for the amount of give in each one. There were five pins and the fourth back seemed to have the most tension, so I worked on lifting that one first. It took me about twenty seconds to get it above the cylinder. The other four took twenty seconds total. I turned the lock with the wrench and it disengaged smoothly.

I glanced at my watch. I had been in there for twelve minutes. *Was I pressing my luck?* I listened carefully. Not a sound except the canal water lapping leisurely at the dock outside. Now for the button lock.

Pulling the door handle toward me, I looked for the curved side of the bolt. It was on the inside. A minor problem. I took from my pick kit a flexible, laminated plastic card with a V-shaped cut in one end. I slid it between the door and the jamb, centering the cut over the bolt. Jiggling the door back and forth, I applied downward pressure on the card. The bolt slid back and the button snapped out. I turned the handle, entered, and locked the door behind me. This had taken about ten seconds, but I was starting to sweat. *The clerk and reinforcements would have to be back soon.*

My light revealed a dirty, cramped cubicle about six by eight with file cabinets against one long wall and a gray metal desk along the other. There was a rolling chair with barely enough room to fit between the desk and the cabinets. Papers were scattered over the desk and some on the floor. I would have no time to get into the files, so I began scanning the papers that were strewn about. An invoice for the masks from Greece listed twenty crates with sixteen masks in each. A big bang. None of the other invoices and receipts were interesting until I uncovered a letter that was in Serbo-Croatian Cyrillic. The name Pakulić was in it. I wanted this. I looked for a copy machine, but then I heard noises from the shop upstairs–the clack of a door, footsteps, and voices.

I looked to the door as the freight elevator whirred into life. No time to get out. I stuffed the letter into my pocket and crawled under the desk just as the elevator gate clanked open. If they came into the office, I was cooked. Someone went to the gate. I heard them cursing out the clerk who had left the loading dock gate unlocked. There were squeaks and grinds of the garage door being raised and the bang of the gate being closed and probably padlocked. I was locked in. *Please don't come into the office.* My hands were sweaty. There were footsteps near the office door. I held my breath. The handle rattled–someone checking to see if it was locked. He didn't notice that only the door handle lock was engaged. No one came in. *Phew!!*

A voice rasped out, "Let's go. We need to find Porello." There were grunts of assent as the elevator gate clanged again and the elevator ground upward. I listened intently as footfalls seemed to move toward the front of the shop. The front door slammed and what I thought was a deadbolt being shot home. *Alone again*, I hoped. I uncoiled from under the desk. The position and tension had cramped my leg. *Ouch.* I slipped my smartphone out of my back pocket and placed the letter on the desk next to other papers with the Soledoro name and logo. I quickly snapped three photos of this arrangement. Then I dropped the documents on the floor. I wanted out of there.

I slipped out of the office, button locking the door. No time to relock the deadbolt. I hoped they wouldn't notice or chalk it up to their own carelessness. I quietly climbed the stairs. At the top, I peered around the corner of the workroom. There was nothing that caught my interest there except the window which looked onto the street. My escape route? If I went out the front door, it would be unlocked and give my exit away. An unlocked window closed behind me might not attract attention for some time and the cause would remain uncertain. Just needed to be sure that no one noticed me leave. It was broad daylight and there were people on the street and in the cafés.

I searched for a prop to explain my egress through the window. There were some tools on the table in the workroom. There was also a painter's cap. I took a screwdriver, and then stuffed my hair under the cap. A six-foot woman attracts more attention than a man. I opened the window, looking around for anyone paying attention. No one seemed to notice. I stepped through to the street, turned back to the window, and poked at it with the screwdriver. I threw the screwdriver into the workroom near the table and closed the window.

Chapter 16

Angela slowed to a walk when she spotted the Soledoro clerk at a *vaporetto* stop. There were other people waiting. She stood at the outer fringe of the throng, hoping she would be able to board the same craft without attracting her quarry's attention. As luck would have it, the arriving boat was empty and could accommodate all the passengers. The clerk pushed his way to the front of the crowd and hopped in even before the *vaporetto* had been secured at the dock. He got dirty looks from the crew members and several of those waiting. Angela was able to board unnoticed and moved to the opposite end of the craft.

The boat motored down the serpentine Grand Canal, making several stops. Angela expected that craft would not empty enough for the clerk to notice her. He was glancing nervously around. *Did he sense he was being tailed?* At the Rialto and the Accademia Bridge stops, quite a few passengers boarded, blocking the clerk's view of Angela.

When they reached Piazza San Marco, the end of the Grand Canal Line, the clerk leapt off the boat and paced impatiently awaiting a Giudecca Canal Line *vaporetto* just about to pull in. Angela held back and was the last passenger to disembark. She knew that the second craft wouldn't dock until the first boat had started its return trip along the canal. She was glad to see that several passengers were intending to transfer to Line 2. Being short and keeping her head down, she shielded herself from the clerk's anxious glances.

At the San Giorgio stop, most of the passengers got off. *What now? He's gonna make me if we get off at the same stop.* At the Redentore stop, the clerk jumped quickly to the landing and headed to his right. Waiting until the last moment, head down, the detective alighted on the dock and turned to the right toward the Santissimo Redentore church plaza. When she reached the plaza of the magnificent edifice, Angela chanced a glance to her left and saw the clerk walking briskly down Calle San Giacomo.

Her target hadn't seemed to notice her. But before striking out in his wake, Angela reached into her well-worn leather purse and pulled out a pair of sunglasses and a beret. She eschewed a brightly colored scarf that she might use for another quick change. She donned her chosen accessories and half walked/half ran toward San Giacomo, finding herself about forty yards behind the clerk. He was moving fast down the street, looking around him at each intersection.

Coming to Calle del Albero, the Soledoro clerk turned left and then right at Do Corte. At the second brownstone on the left, he rapped on a door using its large knocker shaped like a rampant lion with a rising sun back plate. A grizzled older man in a stained smock opened the door after the second knock. The clerk pushed past him with a gruff greeting. The old man shut the door behind him.

Angela waited, standing in the shadow of a recessed doorway across from the brownstone. The quarry reappeared in less than five minutes, carrying a long cloth-wrapped package that could easily accommodate a long gun. He continued down Do Corte, took a right at Calle dei Corti, and regained San Giacomo heading toward a marina at the end of the street.

Entering the marina office, Angela's mark talked briefly with a woman behind the counter, nodded, and exited toward the slip nearest the office. A classic, highly polished, dark wooden speedboat was tied up there. The clerk jumped in and started the engine. The powerful inboard motor thundered into life. He clambered onto the bow and reached to uncleat the painter. The boat slowly backed out of the slip. Once out, the clerk drove along the breakwater to the outlet into the lagoon between La Giudecca and the Lido. From there, he roared off to the southwest, leaving a large wake.

Angela lost sight of the boat very quickly. She frowned and shook her head, then turned toward the marina office and entered. The young woman she had seen through the window speaking with the clerk stepped up to the counter. "How may I help you?" she asked.

"The man who just left in the speedboat. Where was he headed?"

The young woman shook her dark curls and said, "I wouldn't know. We just berth and service the boats here. The owners don't report their excursions to us."

Angela frowned, thought for a moment, and reached into her handbag for a leather wallet. She flipped it open with a flick of her wrist flashing the Venice police ID. The woman looked at it briefly, arching her eyebrows. "How long has the boat been kept here?"

"Well, I've only been working here for seven months, but the slip rental papers seem to indicate a long history."

"May I see the papers?"

The girl sucked her upper lip and narrowed her eyes. Exhaling, she said, "I need to check with my boss. He's not here at the moment."

Angela leaned forward across the counter inches from the young woman's face. The girl recoiled a step. "Look. This is a serious matter. I wouldn't ask you if the stakes weren't high. Just look at the papers and tell me who the boat's owner is and for how long it has been berthed here. If there is any record of where the boat has been going and how often, just tell me. No one will ever need to know where I got the information. You wouldn't want to be considered as obstructing a police investigation."

The young woman pressed her lips into a thin line and nodded. She went to a file cabinet behind her and opened the top drawer. After riffling through several files, she pulled out one and placed it on the counter in front of Angela. Angela opened the manila file cover and saw the latest rental contract. She took out her cell phone and snapped a picture of the front declaration page. The owner was Soledoro, Soc. Turning to the back of the file, Angela found that the boat had been kept at the marina for at least eight years. A copy of the title indicated that it had been purchased by Soledoro from the Constantinides shipping company seven years earlier.

"Do you have any idea where the boat was going today or where it usually goes?"

"Well, since I've been working here, the boat has gone out about twice a week. It seems to usually head southwest and at times the duration of the round trip has been less than thirty minutes. That would suggest that it went to one of the small islands in the lagoon." The girl smiled. She was evidently proud of her keen observation.

Angela returned her smile and thanked her. "No need to mention my visit to anyone," she said with a finger to her nose.

****

Angela decided to backtrack to the brownstone on Do Corte. She banged on the dark oak door with the golden knocker and waited. The sound of shuffling footsteps was heard and a muffled *"un attimo."* Then the metallic sound of the deadbolt preceded the creaking of the door opening slightly.

Half of a grizzled face appeared in the opening. *"Si."*

The detective identified herself as a mask buyer who had admired the master's work at the Soledoro showroom. She smiled brilliantly at the old man and asked if she could see some of his work in progress, or better, watch him at work. Apparently, a modicum of charm and flattery from a lovely young woman overcame any inhibitions he had about being observed at work. Beaming, he opened the door wide and ushered her in. He asked no questions about how she had found him.

He led her by the elbow to his workshop where a long worktable held unfinished masks, tools, paints, and decorative items. On a long clothesline over the table were clipped sketches and drying masks. There were floodlights suspended from the ceiling shining brightly on the table and its contents. More light poured in through a series of skylights in the sloping roof over the workroom. The smell of paint solvents was heavy in the air despite the loud whirring of a powerful exhaust fan and the open skylight windows.

"I'm just now working on a series of masks inspired by Roman mythology. For example, here is a Romulus mask, and here is a mother wolf." He held up the masks for inspection. Angela made the appropriate sounds of awe and appreciation, giving the master another bright-eyed smile.

"Go ahead and continue your work. I would love to watch such a master of his craft. Do you mind talking while you are making a mask?" she asked innocently.

"Oh no. This can be such a lonely and isolating profession. I frequently walk down to the marina, talk to the young woman who works there and stroll along the water. It's good to have some human contact and get away from the fumes of paint and glue. The only people who come by are staff from Soledoro, many of whom don't seem to know or care about masks. And, of course, no one as charming as you," said the master flashing a crooked smile.

"They don't talk to me except to ask if anyone else has been here. I don't quite understand why they come although there is a large meeting room and storeroom in the adjoining wing of this building. It's locked and I've been told not to go in there. I think there's something political going on, but I don't want to know about it. Italian politics–phew! Who can understand it?"

Angela was dying to ask more about the meetings and the contents of the locked storeroom but didn't want to appear inquisitive about the Soledoro crew. Instead, she asked, "Which mask will you work on now?"

Angela risked remaining with the mask maker for another half hour, hoping that the man she had shadowed would not reappear. She learned a lot about the art of mask making and a bit about goings on in the adjoining rooms. When she finally said that she must leave, the artisan's face fell. He recovered quickly, however, thanking her for her interest and saying that he hoped she would return to the workshop.

Chapter 17

Korb was sitting with Treu at an outdoor table in the courtyard of the hotel under a cloudless azure sky and a robin's egg San Pellegrino umbrella. His fork was poised in the air over a colorful *torta rustica* with a golden brown, glazed crust. Treu was twirling linguine with clam sauce around his fork. There were two other chairs at the table. Korb looked up at Su as she entered and cocked his head toward the empty chair to his left.

Su knew better than to interrupt a culinary moment with a report, even though the information she had required quick action. She motioned to a black-aproned waiter approaching from another table.

"*Signorina?*" he inquired, glancing down at her.

She ordered a Peroni and a Caesar salad with Parmigiano custard and Parmesan crisps. Campari had not arrived. Su was uneasy. She glanced repeatedly toward the courtyard entrance. She hadn't seen Angela after the clerk and the gang returned to the shop. The Peroni arrived and Su guzzled it. A bit of relief for her dry mouth. Treu noticed and gave her a quizzical look. The waiter, seeing the empty glass, stopped to inquire if she wanted another. Su nodded. Only when the second beer arrived with her salad did Korb look up frowning.

"Is there something wrong, Kelan?" Korb asked impatiently.

"It's just that I haven't heard from Angela since we

split so she could trail the Soledoro clerk," said Su. Treu glanced up, but quickly lowered his eyes to his plate.

"She'll turn up. Enjoy your lunch," said Korb.

Su stood up and threw down her napkin. She glared at Korb shaking her head. *You cold son-of-a-bitch*, she thought. "I'm really worried. She should have called in."

Korb did not look up but shoveled in another forkful of *torta*. Disgusted, Su turned to leave. As she did so, Campari blew into the courtyard, tousled and breathless.

A little scream escaped Su's lips. She grabbed the surprised Angela and hugged her hard. Campari looked bemused. Su held Angela at arm's length and looked at her. "Are you okay?" she asked.

"Fine, fine. I was just running because I was late. Excuse my appearance," Angela said.

Su turned to look at Korb who raised his head with an "I told you so" smile on his face. She sighed with resignation. Korb had known Angela was on her way all along. The disgruntled assistant sat back down staring at her boss who continued to eat. Su stabbed her fork into the salad and lifted it to her mouth. Halfway there, she stopped and looked at the lettuce. She wasn't hungry.

Korb finished his lunch, took a last sip of wine, and daintily wiped his lips. "Let's hear your report," he said coolly looking at Campari.

Su cut in. "I have to report something that Inspector Mazzini may need to act on immediately." Korb frowned, but nodded.

"I got into Soledoro's loading area. There are

crates of unfinished masks there–all of them made of C4," said Su.

Campari leapt to her feet. "Did they see you?" she asked.

"No and I don't think they know I was there," Su replied.

Campari looked at Korb. "I am very sorry. I must get back to headquarters and get Inspector Mazzini to organize a search. I'll have to give you the full report tonight or tomorrow morning. You got the outline when I called earlier," she said, the anxiety clear on her face.

"Angela, there are twenty crates labeled from the Constantinides Shipping Co.," added Su. Campari nodded her thanks and then gave a tight-lipped smile to Korb before she hurried out of the courtyard.

Treu rose to join her. She motioned him back, telling him to bring Korb and Su along if they wished to be in on the search party. Treu frowned and his shoulders slumped. He returned to the table and excused himself to go to the restroom.

Korb had a rare look of bewilderment on his face. "Well, Kelan," he said, "you seem to have shaken things up a bit. Did you find anything to advance our case?"

Su remembered the letter she had found. Pulling out her phone, she brought up the pictures and handed the device to Korb. "I don't read Serbo-Croatian, but I did note the name Pakulić at the bottom. It was in the loading dock office. What does it say, boss?" said Su with the ghost of a triumphal smile. She took Korb's slight raising of his eyebrows as recognition of her accomplishment.

Korb studied the document, his brow furrowed.

"It's a letter from Pakulić offering his brokerage services on an unspecified, sensitive matter regarding the Bosnian expat community in Venice. He says he will come to Venice to consult with the Soledoro principals and suggests a fee of ten thousand euros plus expenses," related Korb. "He also says that it has come to his attention that these principals have been discussing this matter with a former underling of his and that they should know that she has neither had a connection with him since 2006 nor is she to be trusted. I believe he is referring to Paola Chekova whose picture Detective Campari took."

Korb pulled out his pocket watch. He stood up creakily, using the arms of the chair for leverage. "You and Officer Treu may take the boat and join Campari at police headquarters. I think I'll take a nap. We have plans for tonight, Kelan. I'll fill you in later."

Chapter 18

When Su returned to the hotel two and a half hours later, Korb was just coming out of his bedroom. He was wearing massive, midnight blue, silk pajamas. His bulbous head emerging from the collar had the effect of the moon rising in the night sky. His brow was furrowed and his eyes unfocused. He was clearly still groggy.

"I hope I haven't interrupted your nap," said Su insincerely, thinking the time should have been more than enough. Korb caught the sarcasm, but ignored it.

"The search?" he asked.

"When the cops arrived, there were just two crates of C4 masks. The bills of lading indicated that they'd been misdelivered to Soledoro. They must have been tipped off. Hate to think it was the cops, but who else?" said Su dejectedly. "In any case, there was nothing to connect Golden Dawn with the shop or the masks. They took in all of the employees and went to find the store owner. Maybe they can sweat something out of them."

"We'll have to be careful what we tell the police. Do you trust Campari?" asked Korb, looking concerned.

"Implicitly!"

"If we tell her not to report back what we find, will she comply?"

"I think she will hold back temporarily, but she's a

good cop in a chain of command," said Su

"That will have to do. We need her help," said Korb, closing his eyes and massaging his forehead. Exhaling, he looked up with a slight smile on his face. "Now for tonight," he said. "I had originally thought we would go to the casino, but I made a discovery today that we must follow up."

"Sounds interesting. Where are we going?"

"San Geremia near the crime scene. There are homeless people there who sleep outside most nights," said Korb.

"Do you think they saw something? And will they talk?"

"We shall see. We won't call Treu for the launch, even though I think he is probably trustworthy," said Korb.

"Are you ready for a water taxi?" asked Su looking concerned.

With a grimace, Korb replied, "Out of necessity, damn it."

Chapter 19

Korb and Su arrived at San Geremia around 9:00 p.m. and went first to the Palazzo Labia to seek out Father Ignacio. He greeted them warmly, shaking first Su's hand and then Korb's. "As we agreed, I have not talked to our guests," said the priest. "They have just finished the meager dinner we provide for them and are preparing to settle down outside."

"Thank you, Father. Let's go speak to them," said Korb. The priest nodded and led the two out of the rectory. In the sheltered part of the plaza, there were six people listlessly organizing their minimal possessions around the cardboard boxes and bedding offered by the church. A wizened old man dressed in a tattered tweed sport coat and wool cap looked up, eyeing the arriving strangers suspiciously. He motioned to the others who stopped their activities and gathered around him in a defensive semi-circle facing Korb, Su, and the priest. They seemed to regard the old man as their spokesman.

Father Ignacio stepped forward. "My friends, these people are here to ask for your help in an important matter. I won't insist that you answer their questions, but please hear them out. They assure me that your responses will be held in the strictest confidence." There was a collective show of skepticism—muttering and downward glances at battered shoes.

Korb cleared his throat theatrically and stepped up

beside the priest. "My name is Marko Korb and this is my associate, Kelan Su," he began. His formality elicited a titter from the ragged semicircle. "We would like to ask you a few questions about what you might have seen or heard in the early morning hours of Sunday, May eleven, two weeks ago." This was met with a shuffling of feet and more downward glances. "I assure you that whatever you say will not be revealed to anyone without your permission." There was at least one audible "hah." More may have been stifled by the old man's turning his head and scowling at the vocal one.

Su stepped forward and handed the elderly man a slightly grease-stained, white paper bag. She indicated with a sideward glance that the contents were to be shared. The man took it with a wry smile and glanced inside at the sugar-dusted *chiacchiere*. The rich, sweet smell of the fried, crispy treat brought the homeless folks into a tighter grouping around the old man. He passed the bag around. Each of his compadres reached in almost tentatively and pulled out one of the puffy curls and regarded it reverently before taking a blissful bite. The only sounds for a moment were crunch, the smacking of lips, and a chorus of "mmm."

The old man savored the last piece of his *chiacchiere*, rolling it around in his mouth. He nodded a thank you to Korb and Su. First looking around at his companions and then hard at Korb, he said, "What do you want to know?" There was some grumbling among his mates, but it subsided quickly.

"Two weeks ago early Sunday morning a man was shot near the Campo. Which of you were here that night?" asked Korb.

"I was here and so were Anna, Giorgio, and Fabrizio," the old man replied as he pointed out the other three. His Italian was slightly accented and Korb recognized its Eastern European origin, possibly Serbian. "There were others, but they weren't regulars and I don't know them. They haven't been back since."

"Did any of you hear a shot or shots?" asked Korb.

An unshaven young man who had been identified as Giorgio spoke up. "I thought I heard a shot. I was pretty wasted and was in and out. Don't know if I heard more than one. I also thought I heard a woman scream."

"Did you see anything?" Korb asked.

"I couldn't see where the shots might have come from. That would have been on the other side of the church from us, near the Guglie bridge," Giorgio responded.

"I heard the shots too," piped up Anna, a small, dark, gray-haired woman who looked to be in her sixties, but was probably ten years younger. "There were definitely two. I heard the woman's scream too." Once the ice had been broken, they seemed anxious to talk.

Fabrizio added, "I saw a woman running up the Salita di San Geremia toward the Lista di Spagna, and then two men came by walking fast. I was pretty groggy and didn't get a good look," he said, glancing down apologetically. Anna and Giorgio nodded in agreement.

Korb turned to the old man. "Did you see or hear anything, Signor?"

The man identified himself as Slobodan. "I saw and heard pretty much the same things as my friends. I can tell you that the woman we saw was young, dark-haired, and wearing high heels that clicked on the pavement. One of the men was red-faced, burly, and wearing a brown fedora, which you don't see much these days. The other man was skinny and hatchet-faced with a hawk nose. He wore a checkered cap. Oh, the shots. There was a delay before the second shot."

"Sir, you are most observant," said Korb with a smile. "Can you estimate the time lag between the two shots?"

"It may have been ten seconds," the old man responded.

Korb looked at Su and asked, "Kelan, do you have any questions?"

Su stepped forward and first thanked the assemblage for their cooperation, reiterating that they would not be repeating the information or revealing their sources to anyone. She asked, "Given the ten-second gap between the first and second shots, could the young woman you saw running or the men walking away have fired the second shot?"

"I can't be sure, but I don't think so," said Slobodan, looking at the others who nodded in agreement.

"Did you recognize any of the people you saw on the salita or have you seen any of them since?"

Anna, Giorgio, and Fabrizio shook their heads. Slobodan shuffled his feet and looked at his bedding as if wanting to crawl under the covers and hide. It was the first time he had looked as if he weren't in control of the situation.

Su looked at him, eyebrows raised. "Sir?"

The old man looked up, seeming even older than he had first appeared. His face was drained of color. "I-

I have seen a picture of the burly man in the news," he said. "His name is Perelli or something like that. He's a fascist thug. Big in Golden Dawn. I've run into them before. I don't want to again."

"And the women? Did you recognize either of them?" asked Korb.

Anna said, "I think I might have seen the young one before walking a little dog late at night."

Slobodan, with some reluctance, said, "Yes."

"Thank you very much for your cooperation," Korb said. "It has been most useful. If you think of anything else that might help us, I will leave my local contact information with Father Ignacio. Your parts in helping us will remain in the strictest confidence."

He and Su turned toward the rectory to find the priest and thank him as well.

Chapter 20

KELAN SU

The storm came up as soon as we approached the docked water taxi. The sky grew dark. Lightning flashed in the east, with startling claps of thunder. My first thought was *I hope those homeless folks get inside.* My second thought as I watched the boats rocking on the canal was *Will Korb make it back to the hotel?* I looked at him waddling hesitantly toward the dock, peering nervously from side to side, his breathing quick and shallow. The water taxi was bobbing on the chop. It took both the driver and me to get him onto the craft and into his seat. I couldn't tell whether it was the raindrops or sweat breaking out on Korb's forehead. He gripped the bottom of the seat with both hands.

The ride was rocky as the wind and the waves picked up. Korb was turning green. I was hanging on to my seat as well. I didn't like the way the driver was shaking his head as he tried to ride the swells. Finally, I saw our hotel. The driver looked back with a clenched-teeth grimace. I hoped that Korb didn't see it. The taximan tacked slowly toward the hotel dock, trying to keep from slamming into it. It looked like he would succeed when a sudden, powerful gust of wind drove us hard into the pilings. Korb tumbled from his seat onto the wet deck. While no more than his dignity was bruised, now drenched and queasy, it left him in a foul mood.

It was fortunate that Chef Alberti had set out a cold collation for our dinner in Korb's sitting room. This immediately seemed to help Korb out of the funk that the storm and the collision had put him in. He was about to sit down at the beautifully set rolling table without even bothering to dry off or change his wet clothes.

"No, sir," I said, "you need to get out of those wet clothes. I'm not going to nurse you if you get sick. I'm going to my room to shower and change. You should take a hot shower. The food is cold, anyway. It can wait."

Korb sheepishly agreed and went to his room after a last, lingering look at the table. The lack of any resistance to my suggestion worried me. Did that fall on the water taxi do more than hurt his pride? *I'll soon find out*, I thought, as I headed to my room.

I felt much better after a hot shower and easing into one of the hotel's warm terry cloth robes. As I padded barefoot back down the hall to Korb's sitting room, I hoped that he had regained his equilibrium. I needn't have worried. He was already sitting at the table in canary yellow pajamas chewing a large mouthful of the beef *carpaccio*, pounded thin and marinated in olive oil and lemon juice, and savoring it with half-closed eyes. I didn't interrupt him. I should have known that a good meal would revive his spirits.

I started on the pan-fried scamorza salad. The smooth cheese was dotted with two pestos, one of sun-dried tomatoes, and the other of pureed arugula. The ensemble was on a bed of arugula tossed in a tangy basil vinaigrette and ringed with lightly grilled tomato slices. It was yummy. I looked at Korb. There was a blissful half-smile on his face as he munched on the greens and cheese. He caught my eye and gave me a knowing nod.

****

The late supper and a good night's sleep did wonders for both of us. Korb was dressed, shaved, coifed, and as close to chipper as he ever got, which meant he greeted me with a nod and a curt "Good morning."

A white-coated waiter came in and asked what we wanted for breakfast. Korb ordered his usual: a half grapefruit, creamy mascarpone cheese, a sliced baguette, orange marmalade, and a triple espresso. I ordered orange juice, a latte, a brioche, and grapes. I asked the waiter if they might have some Cantal. That was a French, rather than an Italian, cheese, but my favorite. He said he would ask and if they had none, they would bring the closest Italian cheese. I thanked him.

When the waiter left, I gave a questioning look at Korb. He got it.

"You want to know where we are now in the investigation," he said.

I nodded.

Korb pursed his lips, steepled his fingers, and brought them up to his mouth. "We have too many possibilities: Golden Dawn, Serbian colleagues Pakulić may have betrayed, the mysterious running young lady, prostitutes the victim may have brutalized, or a relative of one he may have killed, any number of people in the Bosnian expat community. We still need to get a line on some of those prostitutes. I also need to talk to more of the ex-pats. It will be a process of elimination."

"Why can't we just leave this to the Venetian cops? It seems to require only exhaustive, routine police work," I said, hoping Korb would agree, but knowing he wouldn't.

Korb frowned. "Kelan, you know that I have made a commitment that I must live up to. You also know that we have already turned up more leads than the police. Furthermore, it appears the police have been infiltrated by Golden Dawn, to what extent we do not know. Finally, the police are frozen out of the Bosnian community. No one there will talk to them while they might talk to me. We are here for the duration."

"Right, boss," I said, hoping the "boss" would annoy him and convey my reservations about this mission. "What's our next move?" I asked with overtones of resignation.

Just then, the waiter arrived with our orders. He apologized for not having any Cantal, but said they would order it and have it the next day. "For today, the chef thinks you might like this Bitto," he said hopefully. "It is an aged, raw milk cheese–cow's milk with a touch of goat's milk. The chef said it has the buttery and nutty flavors of the cantal and is of similar consistency."

I asked him to thank the chef. He bowed slightly to me and glanced at Korb to see if something more was required. A quick shake of the head sent the young man on his way.

Looking at my boss, I raised my eyebrows trying to prompt him to answer my last question. He shook his head again and said, "We'll discuss it after we eat." No surprise there.

When we finished our breakfast, he dabbed at his mouth with a napkin. His eyes narrowed as he gave me an appraising look. I wondered what was coming. Then he smiled slightly and said, "I would like you to confer with Officer Treu. He will be arriving here momentarily. He interviewed several employees of Strega's hotel and looked over the crime scene to see what area residents might have had a view of it. I'm sure you've already perused the police reports of interviews with neighborhood residents. Pick out any of these people you think warrant a closer look and go to see them."

"Right, sir," I said. "What will you be doing, if I might ask?"

"I have some errands to run unconnected with the case," he answered cryptically.

Was that a sheepish smile that flitted across his face? I was sure there was something he was trying to hide, but had no idea what it might be. My marching orders seemed eminently reasonable, although I held out little hope that I would learn much. Anyway, I would be doing something. I can't stand just sitting around.

"What about Campari?"

Korb's brow furrowed. He seemed to be pondering the question. Coming to a decision, he nodded his head slightly and said, "Let's leave her out for the time being. She would be most valuable to us sticking to the Golden Dawn inquiry."

He was right, but I didn't like having to put off Angela. She was now a fast friend and also someone who I trusted to have my back–my first good cop partner.

I nodded and got up slowly. I was still thinking of how to deal with Angela and how Korb was going to get around on his own. I looked at him. He was struggling to his feet no longer paying me any attention.

As I opened the door, I nearly ran into Treu who was lifting his hand to knock. He looked so surprised, I had to suppress a laugh. "Dr. Treu, I presume," I said in English. He shook his head clearly not understanding. "Never mind," I said in Italian. I took his arm and led him back toward the dock filling him in on our assignment.

Chapter 21

KELAN SU

While Treu and I returned to the crime scene in the launch, I asked him about the hotel personnel. He said his interviews had not turned up much. I was particularly interested in who might have left the hotel the night before and early morning of the murder. Treu said that, according to the night desk clerk, there were two bellhops and two maids who left just after midnight. A night janitor saw Mia Strega leave with her corgi around 1:30 a.m. He thought it was late for her to be walking the dog. She usually went out earlier.

"Do we have the contact information for the bellhops and maids who left?" I asked. "It would be good to catch them at home to find out if they saw anything when they left the hotel."

"I have that info in my notebook," assured Treu.

"Good. I just had an idea about how we might get more out of the residents near the crime scene. I gather they were pretty tight-lipped," I said.

"You'd better believe it. I even showed them pictures of Pakulić, the Stregas, and the Golden Dawn duo. They hardly glanced at them before denying having seen anything," Treu said disgustedly. "What's your idea?"

"Do you know the Stregas' Welsh corgi's name?"

"I have it here somewhere in my notebook," Treu said as he riffled through the pages. "The janitor mentioned it. Here it is. Valentino, although they often just call him Tino. Why?"

"People won't talk to you about what or who they have seen near a crime scene. They don't want to get involved, preferring not to put others in jeopardy. But they are happy to help you find a lost pet–no matter where they may have seen it. We believe that the Stregas' corgi may have been around the Campo Geremia around the time of the murder. Let's ask about him."

At first, Treu's eyes widened with surprise and he shook his head, but slowly an appreciative smile crept across his face. The head shake turned into an enthusiastic nod. "Italians love dogs!" he blurted.

"So I've heard." His enthusiasm was contagious. "Is there a print or copy shop nearby? We need to print up some 'lost dog' handouts."

"There is a Digital Copy in the train station at the other end of Lista di Spagna, not far from Strega's hotel."

"Good. We can stop at the hotel and get an authentic description of the dog."

****

CANE SMARRITO (LOST DOG)

Pembroke Welsh Corgi, 2 anni, perso nelle vicinanze di Campo S. Geremia nella seconda settimana di maggio. Nero e marrone chiaro con segni bianchi sul petto e muso appuntito. Corpo lungo, gambe corte, senza coda e orecchie erette. Circa 8 chili. Molto amichevole. Risposte al nome di Valentino o Tino. Se trovato o se hai informazioni, chiama il numero 041. 9146236. Viene offerta una ricompensa.

(Pembroke Welsh Corgi, 2 years old, lost in the vicinity of Campo S. Geremia in the second week of May. Black and tan with white markings on the chest and pointed snout. Long body, short legs, no tail, and erect ears. Approximately 8 kilos. Very friendly. Answers to the name of Valentino or Tino. If found or if you have information, please call 041.9146236. A reward is offered.)

Armed with twenty copies of the notice, Treu and I headed to the apartment blocks near San Geremia. There were three buildings with eight apartments in each. Since Treu had been through the buildings as a police officer, I decided to go in alone while he posted some of the notices outside. This was a good time. Prostitutes would be home during the day and married folks are more likely to sympathize with a young woman seeking her lost pet when their spouses are not present. I thought I'd start on the top floors and work down. I hoped this would work.

I went into the first building. There was no answer at the two apartments on the top floor. On the third floor, I knocked on the door of the front apartment.

"Chi è?" said a tired, raspy, smoker's voice. I couldn't make out whether it was male or female.

"Excuse me, I am sorry to bother you, but I wonder if I could talk to you about my lost dog," I yelled through the closed door in my best colloquial Italian. "Could I please come in?"

"Un attimo," came the voice from within, preceded by a grunt.

I waited and then heard shuffling footsteps approaching the door. It opened a crack secured by a chain. The first thing to appear was a freshly lit cigarette accompanied by a waft of smoke. Next came the puffy, blotched face of a woman who looked about seventy but was probably younger.

"What do you want?" she said looking me up and down.

I put on a pained expression, looking close to tears, and said, "I'm searching for my dog, Tino. He ran away from me not far from here about two weeks ago and didn't come home. There was a commotion on the street, loud noises. He got scared and bolted. I've been combing the neighborhood in case someone saw him or found him," I said, describing the dog and showed her the notice. "Have you seen him?"

The woman's face visibly softened as she looked at the dog's picture. She took a deep drag on her cigarette and briefly closed her eyes in thought. She exhaled the smoke slowly. When she opened her eyes, she said, "You know, sweetie, there was a ruckus near here about two weeks ago. I heard noises too–sounded like shots. It scared me plenty, I'll say. I did look out and there was a small dog running loose." She waved her cigarette hand toward the front window. "But I don't know where he went. Sorry I can't help you more. Haven't seen him since."

"Oh my," I said with a hopeful smile, "this is the first sign I've had of him, Signora…"

"Capobianco," she interjected. I nodded my thanks.

"Do you remember anything else? Other people around who might have seen him or taken him home? It would mean so much to me if I could find him."

"Well, the only people I saw were running away from the Campo. One young woman toward Lista di

Spagna, a prostitute I've seen before toward Rio Terra San Leonardo, and two men walking very quickly past the Palazzo Venièr. Actually, I'd seen the prostitute before. I think she lives in the area. The last time I saw her she had been beaten up pretty good. I guess that's not unusual for such people," the woman said with her lips curled in disgust.

"Do you know her name or which building she lives in?" I asked.

"No," Signora Capobianco said curtly. She was getting tired of my questions despite her initial sympathy for a dog lover.

"It sounds like there was some excitement here that night. Did the police question you?" I asked, trying not to sound too curious.

"They went through the building asking questions, but most of the people here are old. They said that they didn't hear or see anything. We know better than to get involved with the police," she said, taking a long drag on her smoke and starting to close the door.

"Thank you," I said and nodded, turning away. She shut the door and double-locked it.

Chapter 22

KELAN SU

I was hoping that my early success was a good omen, but I had no luck in the rest of the first building or the second building. No one seemed to have seen anything or was willing to talk about it. I also asked about the prostitute who was supposed to have been on the scene and lived in the area. *Nada*, or I should say, *niente*.

My luck improved in the third building. While no one had seen anything the night of the murder, several people knew the prostitute. She lived in a small apartment on the ground floor at the rear of the building across from the concierge. The gossip was that she paid the rent by servicing the concierge and possibly being pimped by him. She was a Bosnian immigrant and lately had been recovering from a severe beating. According to the mailbox in the apartment entry, her name was Mineta Ibrahim.

I knocked on the worn, numberless green door. Nothing. I knocked again louder. I tried yelling her name. Still nothing. I looked around. No one seemed to be curious about the noise I was making. I stepped over to the door marked "Concierge" and knocked vigorously again. I heard some rustling and shuffling inside. A few muffled words. Finally, the door opened a

115

crack and the pudgy, pockmarked face of a man in his fifties stared out at me. "What do you want?" he said gruffly.

"I'm looking for the young woman who lives in the apartment across the hall. She's a friend of mine. She doesn't answer."

He looked me up and down and scowled. "What do you think I am, a social director? I don't keep track of the tenants' comings and goings."

"Really! I've been told that you have a special interest in her," I said, giving him a hard cop look. He actually stumbled back a bit and tried to close the door. My foot was in the way.

"Go away," he said.

"I might be interested in making the same arrangement with you that Mineta has if there's an empty apartment," I said with a sly smile. I hoped it was seductive, but that's never been my forté. However, from the greedy way his eyes narrowed and the leering look he gave me, I guess it worked. He licked his lips.

"What do you mean?" His face told me he knew exactly what I meant and was relishing it.

"Ha," I said, "you knew me from the get-go. But first I need to talk with Mineta."

"Well, she hasn't been home much at night since she recovered from the beating she got. With her face messed up, she needs to troll the darker streets and her johns are few and far between. Even I find it hard to look at her. You can find her most nights behind the casino. She won't come onto the terrace anymore like the other girls. Say, I'll bet you could walk right in if I get you a classy dress. That'd give you the pick of the crop."

His eyes shifted from side to side as a wide, shit-eating grin stretched his mouth almost from ear to ear. He was clearly beginning to count his money from pimping me. "How about a little sample now?" he said hopefully. He stuck his thumbs under the suspenders pulled up over a stained, sleeveless undershirt. Sweat was breaking out on his forehead.

The thought made me want to retch. "No, I need to talk with my friend first. I'll stop by tomorrow to look at the apartment. Don't be scarce, sexy." I batted my eyelashes. His smile stretched even wider than before. Leaving the building, I was smiling to myself. Never thought I'd be able to succeed at the vamp routine–especially with an Italian. I'd find the girl on her track near the casino. We had the casino on the agenda tonight. I wondered if I'd have the right dress.

Chapter 23

KELAN SU

When I returned to the hotel, Korb was waiting. He
sat in a large leather armchair wearing a burgundy
dressing gown, thinning gray hair plastered down on his
scalp as though he had recently showered. He looked
very smug. I had the sense that he had rushed back from
somewhere.

"Was your morning eventful?" he asked. I reported
on my contacts with the building residents and the
concierge. His eyes narrowed in concentration and he
steepled his fingers under his nose, his head slightly
nodding. His lips and nose wiggled from side to side. I
had seen this before when he was thinking hard. It
reminded me of a squirrel contemplating an acorn held
in its front paws. I stifled a giggle.

Korb dropped his hands to his lap. He compressed
his lips into a thin line, his face relaxing as he exhaled.
He looked up at me and said, "Satisfactory work. If this
Mineta Ibrahim Signora Capobianco and the concierge
referred to is one of the prostitutes beaten up by
Pakulić, as I suspect, it is of the utmost importance that
we talk to her. If we can't find her tonight near the
casino, we'll have to return to her apartment." He added
with a sly smile, "Meanwhile, I've had the chef deliver
a light lunch to your sitting room and then you can

prepare for the evening out–an early dinner at Harry's Bar at San Marco and then the casino."

The mention of Harry's, really Arrigo's, made my mouth water. I had been there once before during a college semester abroad. A Bellini, first created there, the fish soup, and the seafood ravioli paraded in their glory across my mind. I guess I was ready for lunch, so I thanked Korb and headed to my rooms.

After finishing the incredibly thin-crusted pizza prepared by the chef, I went to my bedroom anxious about what I would wear for a Venetian Casino evening. I had the basic little black dress and some moderately-heeled black pumps. The string of pearls and diamond stud earrings my parents had given me were my only really good pieces of jewelry. I'd wear my hair up, fastened with an elastic covered with black ribbon. Black and white as usual. I wasn't inspired.

As I opened the door, I did a double-take. My eyes grew large and my jaw dropped open in a soundless scream. There, laid out on the bed, was a bright red, sparkling silk dress–slim sheath, even shorter than my basic black, sleeveless, cut neck high in the front and plunging in the back. An open jewelry case contained a fantastic diamond and blood-red ruby choker, ruby earrings, and a bejeweled hair comb. A pair of shiny, red, six-inch heels was on the floor next to the bed.

Moving closer to gape and inspect these treasures, I felt an excited tremor come up from my gut. They were so out of character. *These can't be for me.* I fingered the material and checked the sizes, recalculating the Italian numbers–*mine.* I gasped. *For me or not, I'm trying them on!! I'll need to get some special underwear for this outfit.* And an uncharacteristic thought spontaneously popped into my head–*or not.*

Korb's mysterious appearance and sly smile when I had returned now made sense. Another uncharacteristic thought struck me–*the darling!*

Chapter 24

Entering Harry's, Korb and Su attracted a lot of attention–not primarily because of Korb's bulk or reputation. Men looked hungrily at Su while women's eyes widened and then narrowed into an appraising scowl. The maître d' and the waitstaff were especially fawning. Despite her lack of experience with such high heels, by leaning on Korb's arm, Su managed to sashay without too much wobble to a corner table and slide into the chair held by the maître d'. When Su tucked her impossibly long legs under the table, the stunned silence that had accompanied their entry returned to the murmur of voices, the tinkling of glassware and the clanking of silver. Men's sidelong glances testified to the difficulty of keeping their eyes off her.

Korb seemed oblivious, looking down at the table and at the menu the waiter had opened in front of him. But an amused half-smile stole across his face as he raised his eyes to Su. She was beaming broadly, basking in the surprising acknowledgement of her striking beauty and sex appeal. Her smile also reflected gratitude to Korb, who had provided the glamorous apparel.

"Shall we start with a Bellini?" Korb asked, unable to keep a twinkle from his eyes. He was pleased that he had successfully challenged Su's disparaging view of her appearance and womanly attributes. Su nodded an enthusiastic yes, and Korb signaled for the waiter.

They dined in relative silence, punctuated only by tasting tongue clicks and satisfied "mmms." It was a light repast as they had work to do that night. Su knew she could afford no bulges in her skintight outfit. They shared an antipasto with a variety of charcuterie and cheeses, stuffed peppers, five kinds of olives on a bed of spring greens and dressed with a light, lemony vinaigrette. Then they each ordered a small bowl of the house's special fish soup. Despite her resolve, Su could not help herself from dipping three pieces of crusty sourdough bread into the aromatic soup. A shared bottle of flower-scented, white Fiore di Campo elegantly complemented the meal. Korb's efforts to restrain himself from snarfing up Su's portions caused beads of sweat to materialize on his brow. He soldiered on.

Chapter 25

Korb asked the water taxi driver to drop them behind the casino near the Santa Maria Maddalena church, an appropriate designation for a church seated on the well-traveled track of women of the night. Korb and Su were looking for Mineta Ibrahim, but they didn't know what she looked like. A number of women in extremely short dresses and extremely high heels passed them eyeing the portly, aging man and the exquisite young woman. The looks were both knowing and hostile, shooting curses at the exotic newcomer who had snatched up a most prosperous-looking old gent.

Korb and Su watched the parading temptresses with some amusement. There was a characteristic strut as the girls paced the street–heads up, chests out, knees slightly bent in the stiletto heels, the exaggerated swaying of the hips, and just enough impact in each step to show off the unconfined jiggling of breasts and booties. There were some twenty women out at this relatively early hour. Korb and Su realized they had their work cut out for them. Korb stopped a dark, voluptuous girl dressed in a skimpy halter top, tight beige silk shorts, and thigh-high boots. "Do you know Mineta Ibrahim?" he asked.

She simpered, cocked her head to the left and looked Su up and down. "You looking for a threesome?" she asked, raising her eyebrows. "I'm available," she said, winking at Su.

Su was taken aback at this interest in her. "Nn-no," she said, "we're looking for Signorina Ibrahim."

"Signorina Ibrahim," the girl said with a smirk. "Here we call her Couscous."

"Is she here tonight?" asked Korb, frowning.

"She usually comes later when it's darker and you can't see the bruises as easily under her makeup. She really got worked over. It's a risk of the trade."

"Do you know how it happened?" asked Korb, one eyebrow raised, leaning forward with interest.

"It was some Serbian guy, one of her regular johns," the girl said. "The bastard didn't think she was dressed well enough to go to the casino with him. He really pounded on her. Left her unconscious and bleeding on the pavement. I called the EMTs."

"Do you know the name of the Serbian guy?" asked Korb.

"No. But I heard he was killed. Hope it was painful," she said through tightly compressed lips. "Say, why all the questions?"

"Will you tip us off when she comes tonight?" asked Korb.

"I don't know. Does she want to talk with you?"

Korb handed the girl a wad of euros. "There'll be more for her when she talks with us. It will be strictly confidential. By the way, what are you called?"

"Angelina," she said with a smirk as she stuffed the wad down her left boot. She nodded and sashayed down the track with an exaggerated thrust of her hips.

Su took Korb's arm and guided him toward a bench near the casino where they could sit and watch for Ibrahim. Su found that sitting comfortably and decorously in her form-hugging outfit was a formidable challenge. From this vantage point, they could see patrons step out onto the casino's rear patio for some air or a smoke. The parading girls made sure to pass indolently by the men on the patio. Some of them watched the prostitutes with interest, but most of the men seemed in a nervous funk, pacing fitfully, head down. This was a losing gambler's usual mien as he contemplated his bad luck.

The few women on the patio were elegantly dressed and looked bored. They were accompanied by oily-looking men who were hovering over them with ingratiating smiles. They spoke in whispers, but the men seemed to be trying to convince the ladies that they would have a wonderful time if only they gave the men more money to gamble with. It was an intriguing show.

After fifteen minutes or so of being the flies on the wall, Korb and Su saw Angelina talking to a dark, slightly built, heavily made up young woman dressed in a miniskirt, halter top, and high-heeled wedgies. Su looked at Korb, who nodded and struggled to his feet. They headed for the conversing pair. Angelina saw them coming and inclined her head in their direction. Ibrahim looked up. Momentarily, she seemed bewildered and rooted to the spot as Angelina took off purposefully down the track. Ibrahim turned to run. She took off in an obviously painful, uneven stride. Realizing she could not chase Ibrahim in her current attire, Su yelled, "Couscous, wait. I have something for you I am sure you will want."

Hearing her street name and the offer, the desperate girl's stride faltered. She stopped and turned, frowning

Lawrence E. Rothstein

with tightly pursed lips. This allowed Su to approach her with money she had extracted from her purse. Seeing the bills, the girl's frown eased, replaced by a wary look. "Oh, you're a customer?" she asked.

"Well, sort of," Su responded.

Ibrahim looked questioningly at Su, one eyebrow raised. Su could see the yellowing purple bruises that Ibrahim's heavy makeup was unable to cover up. One swollen eyelid drooped. There were also multicolored bruises on her arms and thighs. It must have been a brutal beating. Su was surprised that Ibrahim was back on the prowl so soon and that any john would be interested in such damaged goods except to give her more of the same.

Ibrahim's gaze shifted to Korb as he waddled up and leaned heavily on his cane. Ibrahim's expression changed from suspicious to hopeful. The arrival of an older gentleman meant money to her. "*Buona sera,* Signorina Ibrahim," Korb said with a slight, but formal, bow.

"You know my name?" said Ibrahim, with a surprised frown.

"Yes, Miss Ibrahim. I will explain. But first, I believe the custom is to settle the financial arrangements for your services at the outset."

"What services are you looking for? I aim to please," said Ibrahim, awkwardly trying to wink her damaged eye.

"I believe you will find the services we are seeking much less physically taxing than your usual," said Korb with a tight smile. "We are looking for only a few minutes of your time, for which I am prepared to pay five hundred euros," said Korb, watching Ibrahim's eyes follow the handful of bills he extracted from his pocket.

"What can I do for you, kind sir?" she said with a little waggle of her hips.

Korb showed the young woman two hundred euros. "This is for agreeing to answer some questions for us. The remaining will be yours if we are convinced you answered our questions fully and honestly."

"That sounds reasonable. Fire away," Ibrahim said as she reached out for the first installment.

"First, let me tell you who we are and why we are asking these questions. I am Marko Korb and this is my associate, Kelan Su. We are here to assist in the investigation of the death of Stefan Pakulić. I believe you knew him."

Ibrahim blanched at the name. She looked around and over her shoulder as if she were about to run again.

"Now let me assure you any information you give us will be kept in the strictest confidence. We are not obligated to share what we learn with the police. I don't believe you killed the man," said Korb, giving Ibrahim a penetrating look. "But if we are unsuccessful in finding the real killer, the police will find you an easy target for clearing this politically sensitive case."

The woman's shoulders sagged and her head drooped as she grasped the truth of Korb's warning. Almost inaudibly, she said, "Go on. Ask your questions."

"Good, Miss Ibrahim." Korb beamed approvingly at her and handed her the wad of euros. "You are a regular on this track that follows the Rio Terra San Leonardo from the casino to Campo San Geremia. Is that correct?"

"Yes, but I have recently taken a few days off," she admitted.

"Because of your injuries?" asked Korb.

"Yes," Ibrahim answered softly.

"And on the night of the Pakulić killing, you were on duty."

"Yes," she answered with a wry giggle.

"Did you come down as far as the Campo?"

"Yes."

"Were you alone?"

"No. I was with a client."

"Did the client enter the Campo with you?"

"No."

"Why not?"

"There were people there yelling and having some sort of argument. The mousy little guy got nervous. He said he was some kind of aristocrat and didn't want a scandal. Thought the argument would attract too much attention and he would be recognized. He stiffed me."

"So you entered the Campo alone?"

"Yes."

"Why?"

"I don't know. I heard Pakulić's voice. I should have taken off. But I was hoping to see him get some grief from these two tough-looking guys," said Ibrahim, shaking her head at her own foolishness.

"The two men. Can you describe them?"

"I only saw them from behind and I don't see too well since..." she said, pointing at her face. "But one was real big, tall and wide. The other was skinny as a rail and about average height."

"They were facing Pakulić? About how far away from him?"

"Oh, I don't know. They were pretty close. There were also two women there. One between the men and Pakulić, but closer to him. The other was off to the side and seemed to be looking on. Their backs were to me also."

"Did you recognize the women?"

"No."

"Were they prostitutes who frequent this area?"

"They weren't dressed like the other girls here, although one had a good body. The other one would have had a hard time finding any tricks. She was old and dumpy."

"Were the women participating in the argument?"

"Yes, I heard a high-pitched voice screaming something. It sounded to me like 'you bastard' in my language, not Italian."

"What did you do then?"

"Well, I got cold feet and decided to get the hell out of there, particularly after I heard the shot."

"A shot? Did you see who fired it or who was the target?"

"No. I was already turning away when I heard it and I didn't stick around. I'm not that crazy."

"Did you hear any other shots?"

"All I could hear was my feet on the cobblestones and my breathing."

Korb turned to Su. "Do you have any questions, Kelan?"

"Yes, sir," said Su, stepping forward.

"Mineta," said Su, frowning with concern. "That must have been a terrible beating."

Ibrahim looked down and stifled a sob.

"Was it Pakulić who did that to you?"

Ibrahim didn't answer right away. Her shoulders sagged and then she slowly nodded.

"How long before the murder did it happen?"

"Five days," answered Ibrahim, but so softly that Su had to say, "I'm sorry. What was that?"

"Five days."

"That bastard Pakulić was known for having beaten and possibly killing other prostitutes. Did you know any of them?"

"I heard rumors about this being why some of the girls have not returned to the track. I only know the street name of one of the girls–Sarafina."

"Do you know where we could find Sarafina?"

"No. She disappeared. She may be dead."

"I am sure you are glad Pakulić is dead and wouldn't like to see anyone you know get the murder pinned on her. But you must think of yourself. Are you sure you don't know the whereabouts of Sarafina or any of your friends who Pakulić has hurt?" said Su, leaning forward and narrowing her eyes with concern.

Ibrahim looked down to the left and shook her head.

With a hard cop look, Su asked, "Mineta, do you own a gun?"

Ibrahim looked up sharply, clearly startled by the change of tone and the question. "N-no."

"You need to give us more help so we can keep you out of it," said Su.

An audible sigh escaped Ibrahim's lips. "I only know two street names. Sarafina and Bos. They're both out of the life now. I heard that Sarafina was still in a nursing home in Milan. She is deaf in one ear and blind in one eye and might lose the sight in the other. The last

I heard was that Bos was in Munich cleaning in an airport hotel." Ibrahim sobbed, "I gotta get out of this life."

Su said, "One more thing." She brought up her cell phone and snapped a picture of Ibrahim.

"*Che?*" uttered the girl, startled.

"Just so we can check on your story," said Su.

"I told you the truth."

"We're counting on it," said Su. She looked at Korb. He nodded and handed Su the remaining euros. She held them out to Ibrahim who reached for them. Su held on for a moment and said, "Why don't you see if you can use this money to find safer employment?"

The girl grabbed the money with a "hmmmph" and turned to resume her slut strut down the street.

Chapter 26

KELAN SU

After the encounter with Ibrahim, we turned and walked to the entrance of the casino. A spirited din of excited voices greeted us–mostly the winners and those kibitzing. There was a slight hushing of nearby voices and an audible sucking in of breath as we walked in. I couldn't believe that such a response was directed at me, although the light from the impressive crystal chandeliers made my dress sparkle. The fantastic outfit was beginning to feel natural—a second skin. But really, I am too tall, too skinny, too flat-chested, my mouth too wide, and my eyes too almond-shaped to be beautiful. We walked across the plush carpet toward the cashier cages. As people stepped aside to clear our path, gazes remained locked on me. Unreal!!!

Korb bought ten fifty-euro chips. The chips were placed in a black velvet drawstring bag that Korb handed to me. The plan was for me to circulate, look for persons of interest, insinuate myself into the groupings, and learn what I could. I was to bet sporadically, getting conversations started by asking possible informants, most likely male, how to place my chips. Given the male reaction to my new persona, I guess I would have no problem finding men drooling over the chance to instruct me. Korb would retire to the card room for high-stakes bridge. He knew from experience that there were always a few incorrigible gossips in that crowd and he was a life master many times over at both bridge and extracting gems from idle chatter.

"Good hunting," said Korb, as he tapped his cane twice and turned toward the cardroom. Clutching the chips, I surveyed the main hall. There seemed to be a talkative gaggle of bettors at a nearby roulette table. I slowly walked in that direction, stopping just behind a short, chubby man letting a large stack of chips ride on black. A buxom, brassy blond woman and two slim, balding men seemed to be with him as he looked toward them questioningly and they nodded encouragement for his bet.

The croupier called, "*Faites vos jeux,*" and started the wheel spinning. The ball clacked over the ridges. The croupier said, "*Pas de jeux.*" I guess even Italians think French is the language of roulette. The group's eyes were fixed on the wheel as it slowed. The woman gave a "yip" of exultation as the ball stopped on a black number.

"*Vingt-neuf, noir,*" announced the croupier.

The chubby bettor did a little jump and let out a breathy "Ha." As he reached for his chips, the woman put a hand on his arm, restraining him and shaking her head. "Leave them. The only way to beat the damn house odds is to have a lucky streak. You're on a roll. Run with it." For a split second, the man looked as if he would argue. But then he frowned, lowered his head, and pulled back his arm in resignation. The woman and two accompanying men smiled approvingly.

The croupier spun the wheel. The ball bounced

over the partitions. Beads of sweat trickled down the little man's forehead and nose and dropped to the baize. He stared intently at the slowing wheel. His hand went to his forehead as the ball came to rest in a green compartment. He was in shock as the croupier announced *"zero."* He turned toward his three companions with a look of anguish. They were gone.

I stepped in close to the bewildered man. In a breathy voice, I said, "Wow, you are some high roller letting that stack ride. And you lost it without a second thought. Could you help me place some bets?"

He looked down as if he were going to cry. But as his downward gaze seemed to register the length of my legs, he looked quickly up. He pulled a silk square from his breast pocket and wiped his face. When he removed the handkerchief, there was desperation and hope in his eyes. I had made my point.

"Ah, an American. It would be my pleasure, Signorina…?" said the little man.

"Su," I said, beaming with gratitude.

"*Enchanté*. And I am Signor Luigi Luccoccia," he said with a bow and a slight flourish. "But my friends call me LuLu." He looked up at me hopefully. "I fear my luck has run out at this table. Why don't we move on? There is a baccarat table just opening up near the cages. Do you know the game?"

"Not really, LuLu. I watched it once before," I said. I hoped he would interpret my use of his nickname as interest in his friendship.

"It's the game with the best odds. You're not playing against the house. Of course, the house does take a cut of the winnings."

There were three bettors and a dealer at the table.

My gaze was drawn to a tall, elegant elderly woman with silver hair and wearing a silver evening dress. She slid a card face down out of the shoe, a wooden box open on one side containing decks of cards. She then passed it to the dealer, who passed it still face down to another player who had the largest stack of chips on the playing field.

"You see, the game moves slowly with much pomp and circumstance," said the little man. "It makes it a little harder to lose fast. In the States, they play a much faster game, with the dealer pulling and turning over all the cards immediately." The player with the shoe then slid out another card and placed it beside the shoe. The rituals were repeated, so there were now two pairs of cards face down on the table.

The tuxedoed dealer signaled to the tall, slim man with the large stack of chips. "*Giocatore*," he called. The tall man looked at his cards and pushed them, again face down, to the dealer, who finally turned them over for all to see the jack of hearts and the eight of clubs. "*Otto naturale, stare*," the dealer intoned. He then called, "*Banco*."

The silver-haired lady briefly looked at her two cards and slid them with long, graceful fingers toward the dealer. Her magnificent diamond ring sparkled in the light. With a flick of each wrist, the dealer exposed the ace of spades and the six of diamonds.

"*Sette, pagano giocatore*," he announced and proceeded to double the chips placed by bettors on the giocatore line. He raked in the chips of those betting on the bank hand and those who bet on a tie.

"The winner is the hand closest to nine, with face cards and tens valued at zero and the others at face value. Aces are one. If the total is more than ten, ten is subtracted. If there is a tie, no one wins or loses unless they bet on the pareggio line. That pays eight to one. It's a sucker bet because the house commission is much higher on those winnings. There are complex rules on whether a third card can be drawn to each hand. But the game is purely one of luck. There are no skills needed to play–except patience," explained LuLu.

"Well, I guess I'm ready to give it a go," I said, placing my hand lightly on the little man's shoulder. "I want to bet on that grande dame who has the shoe. That means *banco*, right?"

"Okay. Position four is open," said LuLu. I allowed him to guide me by the elbow to that spot. He nodded to the dealer who nodded back.

I took out two red fifty euro chips from the velvet bag and placed them on the banker line above the number four. The other players placed their bets as well. I felt a thrill of excitement as the drawing of the cards began. The player's hand was a four and an ace. The banker drew a seven and a ten. I gave a little yelp. I thought the banker had won with seven against five. The dealer shook his head. I mouthed, "Oh," as another card slid to the player, who looked at it and pushed it to the dealer. It was a seven for a total of twelve and hand value of two. The banker had to draw a card. It was the six of spades. The banker's hand with a value of three was victorious. I was a little confused until I subtracted ten from each total. But why not more cards?

Enough analysis. You're not here to become an expert. I pulled in my chips, beaming at the little man. The silver-haired lady waved her hand toward a young, bearded man standing a few feet from the table. The man moved to her side and she whispered something in his ear. He collected her chips, paid the house commission to the dealer, and placed the remaining chips in a black velvet bag. She smiled at her companion, took his arm, and they sauntered over to the cashiers. I watched them go, hoping I could someday match that elegance.

The shoe was passed to me. I was puzzled and looked at the dealer. He cocked his head and gave me a reassuring smile. He told the players to place their bets. He informed me that I was now the banker and could only bet on the banker line or pass the shoe to the next player. I nodded and placed two chips on *banco*. I looked at LuLu for assurance. He was smiling contentedly, looking a bit like the cat that had swallowed the canary. I pulled the shoe closer, inserted two fingers onto the cards at the open end, and slid the top card out and over to the dealer. I liked the feel of this ritual.

I held the shoe for six hands and had a run of luck. I won a thousand euros. Each time I won I made sure to convey my appreciation to LuLu with friendly glances, words of thanks, and finally with a kiss on the cheek. The little man was beside himself with pleasure. After the sixth hand, I collected the winnings and paid the commission. I squeezed LuLu's hand and said, "That was so exciting, LuLu. Thank you. Let's celebrate with a drink."

"*Certo, Signorina.*"

"Please, I'm Kelan," I gushed, licking my lips and parting them in a half smile that I hoped was seductive. I thought I saw beads of sweat form on the little man's forehead.

He took my arm and squared his shoulders as we marched toward the bar. Many of the other patrons stared quizzically at us, shaking their heads. I suppose they thought us mismatched. In my heels, I was more than a foot taller. LuLu returned the looks with a haughty lifting of his head and regal glances from side to side.

LuLu chose a table in a darkened corner of the room. He held the chair for me as I carefully eased myself into it. *Wouldn't want to split the dress now.* He sat directly opposite, sliding his chair as close to the table as his paunch would allow. If he had been of normal height, our knees would have been touching. A look of disappointment fled across his face as he realized this would not happen. "What would you like?" he said.

"We're celebrating our good luck. How about champagne?"

He smiled approvingly and signaled to a waiter. "Would you please bring over the sommelier?"

"Certainly, sir."

The sommelier, a compact man with a pencil-thin mustache, came to the table and recognized LuLu. "Signor Luccoccia, how good to see you again." He looked me over appraisingly and raised his eyebrows. "Your luck has been good and you would like something special?"

"Esatto, Carlo! A bottle of '02 Dom Pérignon if you have it. If not, an '04 will do."

"For such a distinguished man of taste, we can find an '02," said Carlo with an ingratiating smile.

There was more to LuLu than met the eye. I knew from Korb that '02 was the best year in the last twenty for champagne and Dom Pérignon was a creamy luxury cuvée. But I said, "Please, LuLu, don't order something extravagant for me. In fact, as a big winner with your help, I should buy you the drinks."

He tilted his head to one side and gave me a little smile. "Nonsense, Kelan. My pleasure. It's good to share something I love with a charming friend. And don't worry. I can easily afford it."

While it seemed clear he wanted me to know he was more than well-off, his graciousness seemed genuine. I was beginning to like the little man and felt guilty that my purpose in hooking up with him was solely to fish for information. "So, LuLu," I said, "it seems you are well-known here and well-liked."

He blushed. "Well, much of it is because I like to spend money, but I like to be sociable and I stand by my friends."

A waiter with a silver ice bucket and two champagne flutes accompanied the sommelier, who cradled a bottle in his hands. The ice clacked as the waiter placed the bucket on the table. With a flourish, Carlo showed the champagne to LuLu, who nodded. Wrapping the bottle in a napkin, Carlo twisted the cork and then pried it up with his thumbs. There was a satisfying pop as the cork flew up to the ceiling and landed in the ice bucket. I couldn't help laughing and was joined by LuLu, who said, "Dead center as usual, Carlo."

Carlo smiled and bowed. He poured two glasses carefully, letting the bubbles subside before filling the flutes to the brim. He handed one to me and the other to LuLu. "No need to sample this vintage. I'm sure you'll enjoy it," he said.

LuLu raised his glass, looking me straight in the eye. Another pang of guilt hit me and I looked down, fumbling for my glass. "To a beautiful friend, fine wine, and good cards," he said. I lifted my glass and clinked his, trying to keep my gaze direct and open.

"You are too generous." I pursed my lips. I needed to ask my questions, but I didn't want to bring LuLu down hard. I couldn't help punctuating my comment with a sigh.

"Please, drink your champagne. There's plenty more, and the night is young. Is something wrong?"

His look of concern hit me like a brick. I almost drained the champagne glass in one long draught. "LuLu, I need your help."

"What is it, my dear? If I can do something for you, I will."

Damn, girl, he really is a sweetie. Makes it even harder.

I sighed. "LuLu, I'm not what you think I am." I was stalling. *Get to the point, girl.*

Luccoccia's brow furrowed more deeply.

"I've come here to investigate a murder," I began. LuLu shook his head, bewildered. "My boss is Marko Korb, the detective, and we are here to find out who killed Stefan Pakulić. You may have heard of the murder which occurred two weeks ago."

"Yes, but what does this have to do with me?" he asked, spreading his hands palms up and hunching his shoulders. He clearly did not understand why I had focused on him.

"Oh, you're not a suspect or anything like that," I said quickly. "It's just that, as a regular here, I hoped you might have seen something helpful on the night of the murder. Pakulić was in the casino that night and the murder occurred not far from here."

His downcast look told me that the truth was dawning on him. His hopes for me were dashed. I felt like shit.

He looked up at me and I could swear he was tearing up. "I asked if there was anything I could do for you and I meant it," he said. If anything could have made me feel worse, that was it. But I'm a professional. I had to soldier on.

"Thank you, LuLu," I said. "Did you hear of Pakulić's murder?"

"Of course."

"What have you heard?"

Luccoccia frowned. "Well, I heard he was shot a short way from the casino. I also heard that he used to be a big shot with Serbian intelligence in Bosnia during the war and that he may have been involved in something here," he said.

LuLu was well informed. "Were you here at the casino on the night Pakulić was killed?"

"I was here, but I left early–a run of bad luck," he said.

"Oh." I frowned. I couldn't keep the disappointment from showing in my face or voice. LuLu caught the drift. He looked around desperately, searching for something to hold my interest. I had another pang of conscience.

Suddenly, he looked at me with a hopeful smile. "I have a friend who works here in security. I am sure I can convince him to let you look at the surveillance videos." He nervously chewed on his lower lip, desperate for an iota of my attention.

I couldn't let him down again. The police had probably already seen them but they might be helpful to find out who was here at the same time as Pakulić. I smiled and nodded my appreciation.

LuLu's face filled with a broad grin of relief as he rose from his seat. He came around behind my chair and held my elbow as he helped me rise from my chair. "*Andiamo*," he said, leading me toward the curving marble staircase in the casino's entrance foyer.

LuLu had been modest about whom he knew. He introduced me to Giorgio Sfoglio, Chief of Security for the casino. When he introduced me to Giorgio, he spoke highly of me and asked if the chief could help me out. Mentioning Korb's name immediately piqued his curiosity, and Georgio nodded his agreement.

The head of security was a gruff, burly man. His face was as red as his casino blazer, and he was sweating from constantly pacing along two rows of techs and monitors focused on the casino floor and entrances. He shook my hand perfunctorily, never taking his eyes off the monitors. "I have heard amazing things about your Signor Korb. Are they true?" he said with a wry smile.

I nodded and said, "Only a shadow of the truth. He's a genius."

Sfoglio looked me up and down. "Well then, you must be a *meraviglia* yourself. What do you want?"

I explained that I would like to review all of the surveillance files from May 6 through May 11. "Whew!" he exhaled. "That's a lot of videos. But if you have the time, you can use the set up over there in the corner," he said, pointing to an empty chair facing a computer and monitor. "Start the computer and the video dates are in the Pavid file. Today's password is '*Risorgimento* 13!.'" He turned away and resumed his pacing.

I sat down, switched on the computer, and entered the password. When the screen came to life, I double-clicked on the Pavid icon. The video folders coursed down the left side of the screen and I stopped the scrolling with a click on the May 6 icon. In that folder were forty video files–four from each of the ten strategically placed surveillance cameras. Each camera's files were divided into time periods. One file was from the hours the casino was closed–generally 3:00 a.m. to 3:00 p.m. The other three files divided the working day into four-hour periods. I figured I would start with the 11:00 p.m. to 3:00 a.m. files for each day and skip the cameras focused on employee-only areas.

I took out my cell to send Korb a text about where I was and what I was doing. I didn't expect an answer since he would be involved in his bridge game and his own inquiries. Chief Sfoglio caught my eye as I tapped Korb's speed dial entry. He shook his head. "There's no cell service in or out of the casino–a security measure. If your party is in the casino, I can send a runner with a message. Or you can go outside to make a call to someone elsewhere."

I gave him the message for Korb. I let out a long breath, contemplating the tedious job I was about to begin.

Chapter 27

Su returned to the casino floor bleary-eyed after having endured four grueling hours. She looked around, trying to refocus her eyes. She should check on Korb and report. She had frames copied from the videos of five people who had watched, talked to, or exited either with or immediately after Pakulić on the night of the murder. Three of the five had been at the casino watching Pakulić on the three days preceding the murder. She also had seen a sixth face she recognized. Sadly, it explained why the raid on Soledoro had failed.

LuLu approached and looked at her expectantly. She was surprised that he was still there, but then again... The young detective owed him thanks, but also needed to get rid of him in order to follow up on what she had found. "LuLu, how can I thank you?" she said. "The security videos were a treasure trove."

A broad grin stretched his cheeks, and he nodded vigorously. "I owe you a full explanation of what's going on, but it will have to wait," Su said with a regretful tilt of her head. "Can we meet for coffee early next week and I'll introduce you to Marko Korb and fill you in on how much you've helped us?"

"*Certo, Signorina*," said Lucoccia. He bowed slightly and handed Su a card. As she reached for the card, he grasped her hand and brought it to his lips. "It was a great pleasure to have met you and help you.

Please, call me anytime at the number on my card." With a last wistful look at Su, he did a military about-face and left the ballroom.

Scanning the crowded game floor, Su spotted one of her video finds, watching intently as a large, bald man, also among the photos, rattled dice in his meaty fist. The woman was short and stocky—muscular, not fat. The pallor of her face was accentuated by the scarlet lipstick on her thin lips, and her abnormally jet-black hair. Paola Chekova, the Serbian diplomat, thought to be a spymaster, had been watching Pakulić and talking to Porello and Massimo on the night of the murder. And there she was in person—apparently with Porello, the ultra-right leader. Su stepped up to Chekova and tapped her on the shoulder. The woman turned with a sneer, which faded as she took in the lissome length of Su's body. Her brows lifted with interest as she said, "Do I know you, my dear?"

The older woman's attempt at being sultry was jarring, but Su couldn't let herself be deterred from asking questions. "No," she said. "You don't know me– yet. But I know you, Ms. Chekova."

The Serbian woman's eyes narrowed, but her face betrayed no other signs of wariness. "Well, as a stranger in a strange land, I am surprised and flattered," said Chekova. The flatness of her tone contrasted with the bantering nature of the statement. "And you are?"

"My name is Kelan Su. I am associated with Marko Korb. You may have heard of him."

"Certainly. Of course, I knew him as Mordecai Croboda. But I've had no contact with him for many years."

"I am sure that was to your mutual benefit," said

Su through tight lips. The comment elicited no response from Chekova. Su continued, "Korb and I are here investigating the death of Stefan Pakulić. I believe you knew him."

"I knew him once upon a time, but we long ago parted ways. I don't see what his death has to do with me," said the woman, turning back toward the gaming table.

Su placed her hand lightly on Chekova's elbow to keep her from turning away. Chekova glared at her and attempted to resist, but was surprised by the strength of Su's grip. "Possibly you could help me by identifying some people whose pictures I have?" said Su.

"And why should I help you?" asked the Serbian through tight lips.

"Because otherwise these photos go directly to the Venice police and that might prove embarrassing," said Su. "What can it hurt? Aren't you the least bit curious to see what I have?"

Chekova glanced over at the large, bald man who was now watching her and Su with a scowl on his face. Chekova shook her head when the man seemed to be about to approach. His scowl deepened, but he hung back.

"Okay," said Chekova, reaching over to remove Su's fingers from her elbow. "Let's find a discreet corner in the bar." Chekova gave Su a tight smile and headed away from the craps table. Su followed.

They found just the spot out of sight of prying eyes. They sat down simultaneously, eyes suspiciously locked on each other. "What do you think you have?" said Chekova.

Su pulled one of the pictures from her folder and

slapped it down on the table. It was stamped 06/05/2014; 23:32, five days before the murder. It showed Pakulić and Ibrahim at a roulette table. Ibrahim's face did not yet bear the marks of the beating. Her small stature, short hair, and dark beauty made her appear the gamin. Behind them in the near distance were a large bald man and a wiry, hawk-faced man watching them intently. "Who is this man, Paola?" asked Su, tapping Pakulić's figure.

Chekova raised her eyebrows and gave a slight shrug of her shoulders.

"Don't be coy with me. You worked with Pakulić for many years."

"That was a long time ago. He has changed much since then. I guess that's him."

Su's face twisted into a wry smile. "How about these two?" Su tapped the faces of the large man and the hawk-faced man.

"The bald man is Fabio Porello. You saw him with me tonight. The other is a colleague of his. I forget the name. I met them here recently," said Chekova dismissively.

"His name is Tiziano Massimo," said Su. "They are the top thugs in Golden Dawn."

"Nooo," said Chekova, feigning innocence. "I didn't know that. Fabio was nice enough to instruct me on how to play craps. That's all."

Su pursed her lips, narrowed her eyes, and shook her head slightly in disbelief. "Why do you think they're watching Pakulić so closely?"

"Are they? Maybe they liked the girl? Anyway, what does this have to do with me?"

Su slapped down three more pictures. The first

two, from different nights, showed Chekova, Porello, and Massimo standing close together watching Pakulić. The third one, marked 11/05/2014; 02:10, showed Massimo and Porello on either side of Pakulić linking his arms and leading, possibly dragging, him out of the rear exit. Chekova was right behind them. Su noticed that Chekova flinched slightly as she took in the last picture, but quickly regained her composure.

"It was a gorgeous night to sit on the patio," she offered.

Chekova stood up. "I've looked at your pictures. I think we're done here."

"I'll have to ask your new friends about them," said Su, also rising.

"Suit yourself, honey. But be careful. They're not as tolerant as I am," said Chekova.

Su watched Chekova leave the bar and followed her out. Chekova headed straight toward Porello, who had been waiting nearby. She whispered a few words to him and nodded her head in Su's direction.

Su strode directly toward Porello just as he looked at her with a heated glare. "Signor Porello, I have some photos to show you and some questions," said Su evenly.

"Fuck you!" said Porello with a deadly grimace.

"I think you'd be smarter to answer my questions rather than those of the police," said Su.

"I don't give a shit what you think—and the police, phah," Porello spat out with a derisive chortle.

"Oh, I think we can take care of your police protection. You should check out my pictures. I hear Pakulić really added to your fascist scum's string of failures," said Su with a broad smile.

It was too much for Porello. He lunged at her.

Chapter 28

Korb rose stiffly from the card table and walked slowly to the bar. He was the dummy on this hand and needed a break. "A Fernet Branca," he told the bartender. Its bitterness would be stimulating and fend off the ennui that these untalented players were bringing on. Italian tournament bridge players were some of the best in the world, but not the duffers here tonight.

A red-faced, portly man came up to the bar, shaking his head and muttering under his breath. He ordered a Courvoisier. He was still shaking his head when he looked toward Korb. "Signor, you are new here, yes?"

"Yes, I'm in for business for a short time."

"Well, just a word of advice. I know we get our partners by drawing cards, but try to avoid that man at my table at any cost. Baron di Castello, he calls himself, fake nobility, a snob, and a right-wing ideologue. He's so busy ranting about immigrants, leftists, and southerners that he misses obvious plays and antagonizes the other players to the point that they'll do anything to beat him. Not that it matters much to him. He can't pay when he loses. He only seems to have money for the local skanks. Funny, hates immigrants, unless they're whores. I don't know why they let him in here."

Korb was silent during this unsolicited monologue. He was only half-listening. But when he heard "right-wing ideologue," "local whores," and "immigrants," his eyes widened with interest. At that moment, he was called back to his table for the next hand. He smiled and inclined his head to the talkative fellow and made a mental note to talk to the Baron.

****

Screams filled the air as a commotion broke out in the ballroom outside. Voices rose and fell. Korb was shuffling the cards expertly, riffling them between his pudgy hands. He slapped the cards down with a crack and laboriously pushed himself up from the table. Even with his gimpy waddle, he moved surprisingly quickly toward the door. He was sure that somehow Su was in the middle of the chaos.

Not to worry, he thought. *Su could more than take care of herself. She is skilled in martial arts and trained with a variety of weapons. She is my protection, after all.* He also had confidence in her discretion. Somehow, this did not relieve his concern.

He opened the door to the ballroom and scanned the milling throng of gamblers. Su, at over six feet and in her red dress, was easy to spot. She was standing over a large, bald man sprawled on his back. Her dress was ripped, and her hair that had been pinned up high, had come down. She was poised, ready to strike again. Korb nodded to himself as he approached Su. He was about to ask her what had happened when another man stepped out of the crowd toward them. He had a narrow, weasely, pockmarked face that was contorted into a grimace of intense hatred.

"You fat, meddling fool," the man hissed. "You

and your fucking drag queen Chink whore better get out of Venice or you're dead." Korb was not fazed by threats or insults, but he felt his face flush and sweat break out on his forehead. When the man suddenly turned to Su and spat in her face, Korb lost control. With his teeth bared and ears ringing, he stepped up to the cur and dealt him a tremendous backhand blow to the side of the head. The whop of the blow was audible to the entire noisy crowd, which seemed to exhale in shocked unison. Without a sound, the man sank to his knees and then crumpled face down on the floor.

As the heat of the moment began to cool, Korb was surprised to find that, rather than embarrassment over losing his composure, he was light-headed with elation. Su was looking at him with her eyes wide and her mouth gaping. She shook her head once and slowly a small smile dawned on her face. She moved to Korb's side, put her arm through his, and led him toward the lobby. The murmuring crowd parted before them.

Chapter 29

Outside of the casino, the cool, damp night air was fresher than usual. A stiff breeze came from the east, off the sea, bringing the fragrance of salt water. The police launch was waiting for them at the casino dock. Korb's shoulders drooped as he eyed the lapping waves and the bobbing craft. Officer Treu was catching a snooze when they approached. Su took off her shoes and jumped lightly into the boat from the bottom rung of the pier-side ladder. She shook Treu, who awoke with a start. He rubbed his eyes, taking a moment for them to focus on Su. "Oh, sorry," he said.

"Help me get Korb into the boat," she said.

Su climbed back up the ladder and took her boss's arm. He shook his head vigorously. She spoke softly in his ear. "We must go. I've got a lot to tell you."

The detective looked at her and nodded. She eased him to the ladder and turned him around. Treu came up and helped Korb's right foot onto the first rung and the left onto the second. The ripped dress now allowed Su enough freedom to kneel at the ladder, holding the shaky man's shoulders as he descended.

Once seated in the cockpit, Korb seemed to collect himself. He wiped his forehead with the big silk handkerchief from his breast pocket and straightened his shoulders. He let out a loud breath and asked, "What have you got?"

Su, squatting next to Korb, glanced briefly up at Treu. "Actually, it's what I have to show you. That'll have to wait till we get back to the hotel."

The trip was uneventful. Treu dropped them off at the hotel. Korb even made it up the hotel dock ladder on his own steam. The officer hesitated for a moment, hoping he would be invited in for the briefing, but Korb dismissed him with his thanks. "You must be anxious to get home."

The Venetian cop frowned and nodded. Su threw him the painter and he turned the launch toward the center of the canal.

The long day and night had taken its toll on the huge detective. Korb stumbled as he took his first step toward the hotel. Su moved up close and held him steady, letting him rely on her and his cane for support as he mounted the stairs. They squeezed into the small elevator, almost ejecting the operator. When it stopped at their floor, there was a slight kerfuffle maneuvering to exit. It brought tired smiles to both of their faces.

Korb said," I think we need to postpone your report until tomorrow…I mean, later today."

Su agreed with a nod and a tight smile. "Please let me know as soon as you get up. I don't think I'll be able to sleep much. I have a lot to tell you."

"I also have some new information," said Korb. "Good night."

****

It was noon before Su got the call from Korb. It surprised her because she had been sleeping soundly. "My sitting room," was her boss's curt summons. She rose and dressed quickly.

When she entered the sitting room, Korb was in the

big armchair, still in black silk pajamas. Before him was a cart with a heavy silver coffee service, two cups, two glasses, a carafe of orange juice, sliced kiwi, a tray of croissants and brioches, a wedge of cantal, and a timbale of butter. Su was surprised that he wasn't already serving himself. She lifted a glass and raised her eyebrows at Korb, who nodded. She poured juice for Korb and herself as well as coffee. She helped herself to a croissant while Korb slathered butter on a brioche. They each savored their first bites, chewing slowly.

Korb swallowed first. He took a sip of juice, then coffee, and finally looked hard at Su. "Report."

Su picked up the envelope she had placed on the floor. "I met a sweet guy at the Casino who taught me how to play baccarat. I won a thousand euros."

Korb frowned. "Commendable." He closed his eyes and shook his head. "And?"

Su smiled to herself, enjoying the pique she had aroused. "This guy introduced me to the security chief at the casino. I spent several hours looking at security camera videos and found some interesting things."

"Didn't the police check out the videos?" asked Korb, his brow wrinkling.

"I'll get to that, Chief," said Su, ignoring his grimace. "Here are some of the pictures I copied off the videos." She slid them out of the envelope. "I looked at videos from five nights before through the night of the murder." The associate pushed aside dishes and placed three of the photos in front of Korb. They showed Massimo, Porello, and Chekova apparently conversing with each other while watching Pakulić. The detective looked closely and nodded his head. Su swept the first batch of pictures to the side and slapped down the one with Pakulić being dragged out.

Korb looked up, his lips pursed and his eyes wide. A guttural "hmmph" escaped from deep down in his throat. There was a question in it. Su had the answer. She slapped down another picture. It showed a young man surrounded by a group of smiling people getting a clap on the back from one of them. The group was Massimo, Porello, and Chekova. The young man was Officer Treu.

Korb exhaled. "That answers more than a few questions," he said.

Su half lowered her eyelids and said, "According to the security chief, it was Treu who came to look at the videos for the police. Apparently, he reported that he found nothing of interest."

"That's why there were no casino pictures in the police file," said Korb. "Undoubtedly, Treu was also the one who tipped off Golden Dawn about the Soledoro raid."

Su gave a dejected nod of agreement. "So much for my judgment about his politics."

Korb gave a short laugh. "Don't bother yourself about that. Politics around here is very complicated."

"Don't I know it," said Su with a snort. "You said that you have some new info too, Boss."

"Will you please stop with the 'Chief' and 'Boss'? You know I don't like it. Korb or Marko will do," said the corpulent detective, shaking his head.

"Right Bo-K-Korb," said Su, screwing up her face in feigned embarrassment.

Korb inclined his head acknowledging her effort. "Now, to the point. I told you that bridge players were notorious gossips. All I needed was to lend a sympathetic ear. One of the players dished about a penniless fake Baron who likes to patronize immigrant prostitutes. Of course, he was more intent on criticizing the Baron's card play and asinine table talk."

It was Su's turn to be impatient, but she held her tongue, not wanting to antagonize her boss. She leaned forward and moved to the edge of her seat, hoping the man would get the "cut to the chase" message.

"It so happens that this Giorgio Tedesco, who calls himself Baron Di Castello, was in the casino on the night of the murder. However, he spotted someone to whom he owed money coming his way. He made his escape to the patio at the rear of the building. One of the bridge gossips said that he hid behind a potted plant." Korb chuckled. "He apparently has little concern for his dignity when it comes to avoiding creditors."

Su wriggled impatiently in her seat. "So did this Baron see something important?" she asked.

"Kelan, you must allow me to tell this in my own way."

Su nodded as her hand went to her face, hiding her eyes. "Sorry, sir. I guess you know how anxious I am to finish up here and get back to Chicago."

"No more than I," said Korb with a tight, sympathetic smile. "Okay, it turns out that Tedesco was the client who was with Ibrahim on the night of the murder. He is one of her regular johns. He didn't simply run off. He hid behind the corner of a building and watched what was going on."

"How did you find all this out?" asked Su, agape with amazement.

"A little flattery goes a long way with someone who has an inflated image of himself as a bridge maven. He also needed little encouragement to disparage Ibrahim as a shrewish slut who was dying to see her abusive, former boyfriend get his. He says that she didn't turn away before the first shot. She kept walking slowly toward the scene," said the big man, slapping his hand down on the cart, causing the dishes and the silver to jump with a clank.

"We'll have to brace her again," said Su, frowning. "I know where she lives if we don't find her at her usual post. What else did Tedesco see?"

"He says he did leave after the first shot. That first shot came after the gun seemed to have been dropped or knocked down and he heard a second shot several seconds later. He also says that while he was watching, there were two women and two men confronting a third man. One of the women, the younger one, ran off after the first shot. He didn't see any other effect of the shot. He also says he couldn't identify any of the people. That's his excuse for not going to the police."

"Should we get him in to the Inspector?"

"He'll deny it all, although I imagine, he could be sweated into some admissions. I don't think he can add anything to what he told me," said Korb, shaking his head. He reached for his coffee cup, took a sip, and made a face.

Su picked up the silver pot and offered Korb a warm-up. He nodded, and she filled his cup. "What's our next move?"

Korb looked up at the ceiling and closed his eyes. He raised his fingers from resting on the cart. "I need to see Strega again and talk to his daughter. We need some straight answers from them. I'll need to push her. We know Mia Strega's story is untenable, given what the people we've talked to have said." His eyes narrowed. "You will need to confront Ibrahim and find out what she saw after the first shot. Bring Campari with you. I think she'll need to take Ibrahim into custody as a material witness, otherwise, the girl might bolt."

"When do we start?" asked Su.

"You start today with Ibrahim. Tomorrow I'll tackle the Stregas. I have an appointment in Trieste this afternoon," he said with an enigmatic half smile.

Chapter 30

KELAN SU

I called Treu's cell number. I thought it a good idea to keep him close, both to watch him and to let him think he was still trusted. He said he was working on another case in La Giudecca, but was about to return to the station. He was nearby and could pick me up on the way. He seemed very anxious to stay involved in our case. It made me think that he might be on the island to report to Golden Dawn, as that was where the Soledoro master mask maker worked. Outsiders were quickly identified. It would be a good place for the fascists' headquarters. It might be worth it to raid that workshop at some point.

I then called Angela. I told her that we were going to possibly arrest Ibrahim. She had lied and witnessed more than she had admitted to Korb and me. We'd pick her up at the commissariat in the launch. Angela was also anxious to meet me as she was mired in paperwork and longed to get out.

It was a sunny and warm day and the lagoon was a bright blue. I was standing at the dock enjoying the gorgeous day when the launch arrived. Treu waved a greeting as he approached. I sketched a wave in return. As the boat pulled alongside the dock, he threw me the mooring rope. I tied it to the cleat with a slipknot and went down the ladder. The officer reached up to grab my arm and help me get into the boat. On the way, his other hand slid a bit too searchingly across my thigh. I clamped my jaw shut to keep from saying something, but I couldn't resist a cold glare as I turned to face him. He seemed to get the message as he dropped his gaze to the deck and took a stumbling step backward. I hoped he didn't sense that my distrust and dislike went beyond the fumbling.

"We're going to the station to pick up Campari," I told him. He nodded.

"And then?"

"Ibrahim's place."

"Why?"

"She lied to Korb and me. Saw more than she said. We'll pick her up and let her think she's a murder suspect."

Treu frowned as he turned to the controls and signaled to me. With a flick of my wrist, I released the mooring rope and gathered it in. We sailed away into the canal; the wind blowing across my face as I inhaled the salty air. I closed my eyes, savoring the moment. It was a cleansing ritual.

When we arrived at Campo San Zaccaria, we were told that Angela was in the squad room. We found her at a metal desk covered with forms. She seemed completely exasperated as she searched for something in and under the pile of papers. She didn't look up right away as I stood in front of her desk offering a sympathetic smile. When she finally saw me, she let out a sigh of relief.

Angela jumped to her feet, grabbed her purse, and practically shouted, "*Andiamo*." I couldn't quite stifle a chuckle at her evident joy at being liberated. Leading the way to the door, she grabbed the handle. Before opening it, she looked back at me and asked, "So where are we headed?"

****

In fifteen minutes, we were standing in front of Ibrahim's green door. I raised my hand to knock but quickly drew it back. There might be a back door or a window opening on the street behind the building. My first thought was to send Treu to check and to wait there in case Ibrahim bolted. But with Treu's link to the Golden Dawn crew, I was worried that he might prefer that Ibrahim had no truck with us. I needed to keep my eye on him, so I asked Angela to go around to the back. Her brow furrowed as she looked a question at me. I pretended not to get it. We gave her five minutes to get into position.

I looked at Treu and he nodded. I rapped hard five times on the well-worn door. There was no response although I thought I heard movement within. I knocked again louder. I yelled at the door, "Mineta, it's Kelan Su. Remember my boss and I had some questions and gave you money yesterday?" I heard what sounded like a window being raised and exchanged a look with Treu. I jerked my head toward the door. He took my meaning and was about to deliver a kick when we heard a scream and a stream of profanity. Treu followed through with his kick. The door shuddered but held. I was about to take my turn when the door opened and Ibrahim appeared in the doorway with Angela right behind her. Angela had a hammerlock on Ibrahim's arm as she pushed her through the door toward us. Ibrahim's face was screwed up, flashing me a look of intense hatred.

"These are police officers and you are under arrest," I told her.

"You said you'd keep me out of this," Ibrahim whined.

"*If* you were straight with us."

"You fucking bitch," she hissed. She wriggled, trying to shake off Campari's grip.

"Hold her out here. I want to look around the apartment," I said.

The apartment was tiny, about 90 square meters. It stank of spoiled food, cheap wine, sweat, and mildew. Dirty dishes, pizza boxes, empty bottles, and clothes were scattered everywhere. Treu and I donned latex gloves and picked our way carefully through the debris. I noticed a framed picture of a younger Ibrahim. Her small stature, short hair, and dark beauty was striking. It made me sad to think of her present bruised and derelict state.

The only other thing I found of interest was a wad of bills rolled up and rubber banded with a note that read, "P.C., 5207777, 15:00, 16.5, *Ferovia*." I carefully slipped the bills and the note into a plastic evidence envelope and put it in my shoulder bag. I had a hunch Korb would find it useful. Treu came up empty. I was keeping my eye on him. He didn't seem to miss or hide anything important. We left, locking the door behind us. The air in the hallway was marginally better, and I breathed deeply for a moment.

The fight had gone out of Ibrahim. She stood, shoulders stooped, leaning her head against a wall. Her cheeks were wet. Angela had let go of her armlock but was watching her closely.

"Okay. Let's take her down to headquarters." Turning to Ibrahim, I said, "This time we're gonna stick you with a murder rap." She whimpered as Campari and Treu led her to the launch.

Chapter 31

Korb asked to have an early light lunch brought to his sitting room. When it arrived, he was still lost in thought about his afternoon rendezvous in Trieste. Uncharacteristically, he only picked at the schie with polenta, granseola, canoce, and the other fried seafood tidbits. Not only was it going to be a ticklish negotiation, but Trieste, on the border with Slovenia, was as close as Korb had been to Banja Luka since his escape.

Korb chose his wardrobe carefully in order to attract as little attention as possible for a three-hundred-fifty pound behemoth. He had rounded up a scuffed and well-worn pair of work boots, navy blue wrinkled chino pants, and a ratty, grey fisherman's sweater. He topped it off with a Greek fisherman's cap. This last was his one concession to style. The cap matched exactly the navy blue of his pants and was trimmed with a gold braided hatband. Korb excused his vanity by using the hat as the identification signal to his contact. Regretfully, he realized he'd have to leave his cane behind. It was altogether too conspicuous and out of character with the rest of his wardrobe.

Hoping that the staff and any other guests would still be at lunch, Korb peered out from his doorway, scanning the hallway to the left and right. No one. He moved quickly to the empty freight elevator at the end of the hall. Instead of descending to the ground level, Korb pressed the S button. That would take him to the basement and the wine cellar. He knew there was a bulkhead door for deliveries. The elevator started with a jolt, whirring and clanking its way down. With the staff at lunch, he counted on no one else using it.

He reached the cellar without being seen. There was some bustling about where some of the hotel's provisions were stored, but he was able to edge his way along a wall to the bulkhead door. The door opened quietly and Korb laboriously climbed the short flight of stairs that led to a back courtyard used for parking and unloading service vehicles. No one was in sight as he exited through the gated driveway.

Sweating and wheezing, the rotund detective sighted a bus stop bench and sat down to collect himself. He had forty-five minutes to get to the train station. Korb called a water taxi service. That should get him to the station in thirty minutes or less. He requested the taxi to not pick him up directly in front of the hotel, but several meters down the quai nearby. He dreaded the thought of another boat trip, but it couldn't be helped. Nevertheless, he was almost looking forward to the train ride to Trieste. He much preferred traveling in relative comfort on solid ground, or better yet, not to travel at all.

When the water taxi arrived ten minutes later than he had expected, Korb was obliged to board hastily. The reluctant passenger closed his eyes and took the fateful step off the dock. He landed in the boat thanks to the guiding hands of the taxi driver. His knees buckled slightly under the strain of carrying his tremendous bulk. The boat dipped, and water splashed over the gunwales. The driver helped him to his seat, shaking his head. Only after being seated did Korb open his eyes.

With great reluctance and trepidation, he said, "I have a train to catch in twenty minutes at Mestre. Speed is of the essence."

The driver raised his eyebrows and rounded his lips in a silent whistle. Having consigned his fate to the boatman's skill, Korb gripped the partition in front of him with white knuckles as the boat turned into the current and began to accelerate.

A more intrepid traveler might have enjoyed the exciting ride. The taxi sped across the water like a jet ski. The slight chop that had been raised by the wind made the boat bounce and slap rhythmically. The boatman weaved skillfully in and out of the canal traffic. They made it to the central train station with ten minutes to spare. Once out of the boat but with his knees still wobbling and his hands shaking, Korb forked over several bills that included a healthy tip.

"*Buona fortuna*," said the boatman.

Korb nodded and turned shakily toward the station entrance.

The station was bustling, but Korb was lucky to find a ticket window without a line where he bought a round-trip ticket to Trieste. He had three minutes to get to the platform. Korb gathered his strength for a brisk walk to the train and was helped aboard by a conductor. He mounted the stairs panting only seconds before the train began to move. The detective edged his bulk down the corridor toward an empty compartment. He only had to squeeze past one man in the aisle who was looking out the window. Korb mumbled an insincere "*scusi*" as he slid open the glass compartment door. He collapsed into the forward-facing bench seat, took off his hat, and mopped his brow with a large white handkerchief. The door slid closed and Korb hoped he would have the compartment to himself for the two-hour trip to Trieste.

The rider's mood improved as the train gathered speed and his breathing returned to normal. He was very fortunate to have a reliable contact in the Serbian consulate at Trieste. Bogodan Slivitz had been one of the few Serbian diplomats who had tried to stop the war atrocities and who had demonstrated good faith in all his dealings with both Bosnia and the West during the war. The third class posting in Trieste was his "reward" for not being sufficiently partisan. Korb hoped his meeting with the man would not attract the attention of his superiors.

As the train passed the halfway mark, Lignano Sabbiadoro, clouds began to gather in the south over the Adriatic. This worried Korb. Rain would make anyone out at the designated meeting place more conspicuous. It might also discourage his contact from going to the meeting. Korb had no way of changing the meeting site and he certainly couldn't show up at the consulate. He had not thought to bring an umbrella, having left Venice in the brilliant sun. He should have remembered just how rapidly the weather over the Adriatic could mutate. He hated being out in inclement weather. In fact, he hated being outside.

When the train pulled into the Trieste central station, the clouds were thick and gray, the air electric and heavy with humidity. A thunderstorm was in the offing. Korb descended gingerly from the car, gathered himself, and walked stiffly to the taxi stand. There was a line. He cursed under his breath.

Just as he moved to second place in the roped-off queue, a young woman in a short skirt and incredibly high heels elbowed her way past Korb and a tiny elderly lady in tweeds holding two well-worn suitcases. The little lady gave a short scream, lifted one brogued foot, and planted it firmly on the young woman's backside, sending her stumbling into the sagging rope. The older lady turned to Korb and motioned for him to follow her past the fuming woman struggling to right herself and recover her rolling bag.

The surprised and amused man couldn't help smiling and congratulating the woman on her marksmanship. Korb remarked that he had seldom seen justice so quickly and efficiently carried out. The woman's face crinkled into a tight smile and said, "These young ones need to be taught respect for their elders." He nodded his agreement.

"Madam, I am only going a short way. If we could share the next taxi, I will gladly pay the fare to your destination," Korb ventured.

"And where are you going?" the woman asked.

"To the Giardino di Villa Cosulich."

"That's not far, but it looks like rain."

"That's why I'm in a bit of a hurry."

The woman agreed just as the next taxi pulled up to the line. The taxi driver got out and placed her luggage in the trunk. He looked curiously at Korb who had no bags. Korb opened and held the curbside taxi door for the lady. She slid quickly into her seat, again belying her apparent age. The courtly detective shut her door and moved to the street side, waited for a car to pass, opened the door, and laboriously crammed himself in without encroaching too much on the woman's space. They gave the driver their destinations and Korb said he would pay the woman's fare as well. The detective pegged the cab man's accent as probably Slovenian. Settling back in their seats, the passengers lapsed into a comfortable silence.

As the taxi proceeded up Strada del Friuli, fat spits of rain splatted on the windshield. Korb became anxious, but it appeared to be only a squall line. Despite the darkening sky, the rain had stopped by the time the cab reached the park. Korb pulled himself out of the taxi with both arms, trying unsuccessfully to suppress a grunt. He paid the driver and saluted the old woman who smiled back, inclining her head. He looked around. Just up the road was the Serbian Consulate. He saw no one on the street or at the park entrance. He hoped the threatening storm would keep consulate personnel from taking an afternoon stroll.

Korb began a slow walk down the central avenue, past well-tended greenery toward the villa. There seemed to be no one about. He glanced nervously at the sky. Dark, but no more rain. When he reached the circle surrounding a reflecting pool, Korb went to the right and found a narrow path leading to a wooded area. Sitting on a wrought-iron bench about 100 feet ahead was a man with one leg crossed over his knee. The detective could not immediately tell if it was his contact, whom he hadn't seen for many years.

As Korb neared the bench, he avoided staring at the occupant. The man only glanced briefly in his direction. Korb was about to conclude that this was not his contact, when he heard, "Are you looking for someone, Signor Korb?"

Korb realized that this gaunt, gray, tired-looking, old man was indeed Bogodan Slivitz, the athletic, dashing, playboy diplomat who had defied expectations by being the most humane and honorable Serbian official Korb had encountered during the war.

"Bogodan," Korb almost yelped. "I didn't recognize you. How did you know it was me? Was it the hat? I'm not exactly the one hundred sixty-five pound marathon runner you knew so many years ago."

"Ahh, Marko, you forget you are famous. I have seen your picture many times in recent years."

Korb sniffed and shook his head. "Even those pictures, or should I say picture, are misleading. They use the same one from the Hallberg case. It's been at least ten years since I gave anyone a photo opportunity. But how have you been? I can tell that the Trieste Consulate is not exactly a plum assignment."

"How right you are. I am not to be fully trusted because I warned against committing war crimes. It is hard for me to understand how so many of my beloved countrymen turned from being the cement of a multiethnic society into rabid supporters of ethnic cleansing."

"Why do you stay?"

"Why does anyone stay with the familiar? My family. I have a job, such as it is. I am too old and tired to start over elsewhere. But what is it that I can do for you?"

"I think you must know why I am in Italy, Bogodan," said Korb, his eyes narrowing.

"Yes, the Pakulić murder."

Korb lowered his head.

"And what do you want of me?" asked Slivitz. He

frowned and his lips pressed tightly together.

"Are you aware of Paola Chekova's presence in Venice?"

"I am," responded Slivitz as he uncrossed his leg and shifted in his seat.

Korb lowered himself carefully onto the bench. There was a slight clang. Korb turned to Slivitz. "Do you know why she is in Venice and, most particularly, what her relationship to Pakulić is or, rather, was?"

Slivitz looked up, frowning. "Let me try to answer your second question first. You know Chekova worked for Pakulić during the war. It's said she was his right hand in spying operations, although her official position was minor."

Korb nodded.

"It's also rumored that they were lovers despite both being married to others. Neither spouses survived the war, dying under somewhat suspicious circumstances. After the war, they lived together until about seven years ago. Pakulić had become more and more dissolute and was constantly in the company of whores. They fought. He threw her out. From that point on Chekova seemed to be stalking him—constantly showing up where he was and doing what she could to disrupt his plans."

Korb exhaled. "That seems to answer my first question too. She followed Pakulić to Venice and got involved in his plans in order to sabotage them."

The diplomat shrugged.

"Does Chekova have any diplomatic status?" asked Korb.

Slivitz looked dismayed at this tack, hesitated, and then nodded. "She isn't listed on Cerionline, the Italian

Diplomatic Protocol database. Of course, given the extent of trade and travel between Serbia and Italy, it is in my government's interest to prevent any Serbian connection to Italian ultra-right actions. It's possible that there was some unofficial encouragement for her to block Pakulić's activities."

Korb nodded, paused, and then looked hard at Slivitz. "Bogodan, are you in a position to access the Cerionline database and add Chekova to the consular mission staff accreditation?"

The furrow in the diplomat's brow deepened, hooding his eyes. He did not respond immediately. He inhaled and exhaled deeply. "Marko, I have the credentials and password for accessing the Italian diplomatic protocol online service. But my job would be at stake without the Head of Mission's authorization. I know I owe you for what you did for my sister and her family, but you'll still have to give me another very good reason."

Korb leaned toward his contact. "I would never presume to ask for a quid pro quo for helping a friend and a desperate refugee, Bogodan. As to a good reason that might benefit your government, I have some very definite suspicions. But I don't want to tell you what they are until I am sure. I also won't ask you to do anything until I have verified my suspicions. I hope I can save your government serious embarrassment that would occur if it knew about and did not try to prevent a devastating act of ultra-right terror. Serbia's chance of joining the EU would be severely compromised."

Slivitz, who had been on the edge of the bench, slumped back, his head lowered and his eyes closed. He seemed to have aged several years during the course of this conversation. A small sigh escaped his lips as he looked up again. "Okay, Marko. I'll have to trust you to limit the collateral damage to Serbia and me. How will you contact me when the time comes?"

"As you know, I found your personal cell phone number. May I use that again? I will call from a public phone and keep the call cryptic and short."

"All right," said Slivitz, shaking his head.

Korb reached over and lightly grasped the diplomat's shoulder. He gave Slivitz a tight-lipped smile. "Thank you, old comrade. You know I will do what I can to avoid compromising your position."

The diplomat stood up. Korb thrust himself up with his hands. They exchanged information for the next contact. Slivitz took out his business card and wrote on the back, "This man has my trust. Listen to him." Korb took the card, thanked Slivitz for working with him, and shook his hand. Slivitz suggested that Korb leave first. Korb nodded and turned to leave. His old war-time acquaintance added, "Well, old friend, after this, I may be seeing you in Chicago and asking you for a favor."

Korb turned back momentarily, nodded, and saluted.

Chapter 32

Korb's reentry to the hotel was uneventful. He quickly let himself into the suite. Korb wondered if his precautions against recognition had been necessary or effective. He hadn't wanted to be followed to his contact.

Su had not yet returned from her rendezvous with Ibrahim. Korb undressed in his bedroom and moved on to the bathroom for a shower and shave.

After donning his tailored pin-striped, gray double-breasted suit, off-white shirt, and blue paisley tie, Korb felt more himself. He checked the mirror, brushed his hair, and straightened his tie. Slipping into the tasseled black loafers was much easier than the struggle he'd had getting his charcoal gray socks on. It was no piece of cake for him to reach down to his feet. He had a special tool at home for this, but had forgotten to bring it. While the clothing was elegant, Korb still looked like an aircraft carrier standing on end.

There was a knock on the suite door. Korb assumed it was Su, who had a key card for the suite sitting room. He said, "Come."

Without any greeting, breathless, she blurted out, "Ibrahim's in custody."

Korb looked at her with a curious squint. "How long can they hold her without charges?"

"Ninety-six hours."

Korb nodded. "Good. Let's go to dinner."

****

During the sumptuous meal at a restaurant near the Lido that Chef Alberti had recommended, Korb's brain pulsed with activity. He felt entirely justified in having an extra order of breaded artichokes. After all, he had not eaten much lunch during an extremely physical day. Su watched with a mix of disdain and admiration, and possibly a little envy, as mounds of food disappeared off Korb's plates, washed down with two bottles of fine wine.

After the voracious gourmet finished the last drop of his limoncello, he daintily wiped his lips with the starched white napkin. He looked at Su, who couldn't stifle her "mmmmm" or resist patting her full stomach. His eyes widened and a slight smile cracked the edges of his mouth. "Let's get back to the hotel and go to work. We are at the endgame," said the satisfied, fat detective.

****

Korb was comfortably ensconced in a large leather wing chair, while Su sat across from him on the edge of the seat of a wooden rocker. Her hands were in her lap, focusing intently on her boss, who looked to be in a trance with his fingers steepled under his chin and his eyes half closed. Su cleared her throat softly.

Korb's eyes shot open. "What have you to report about the arrest of Ibrahim?" Korb questioned, frowning.

"It went all right. She tried to bolt out a back door, but Campari was there and took her in without incident. I kept Treu with me. Couldn't be sure what he might do."

Korb nodded with a far-off gaze.

"I told Ibrahim that we know she lied to us and she might be charged with the murder. That broke her down pretty fast. I found something interesting in the apartment." Su reached into her shoulder bag and produced a plastic envelope with the wad of bills and the note she had found. Su handed the evidence envelope to Korb, who took it gingerly.

He extracted the wad by inserting a pen from his breast pocket into the side of the roll of bills. "Did you count the money?"

"Not yet. But I estimated about one thousand euros. I wanted you to see it as I found it."

Korb made a slight growling assent from deep in his throat. He looked at the note. "P.C., 5207777, 16.5, 15:00. *Ferovia*. May 16th was five days after the murder; fifteen hundred hours, three p.m. the time. And the number?"

"It's a local telephone number. Campari ran it. It's registered to a *pensione* in the Dorsoduro. You'll never guess who's staying there."

"Come, come. That's easy. P. C., Paola Chekova," said Korb with a smirk.

Su sighed. "Yes. Sir, how would you interpret this find?"

"I would say that Ms. Ibrahim is blackmailing Ms. Chekova about something she saw on the night of the murder. I assume you agree."

Su's lips tightened as she nodded.

Korb's faraway look returned. His left forearm, elbow resting on the arm of the chair, fist lightly closed, moved back and forth. For a moment, he stared at it as if it belonged to someone else. "I think we can use this to our advantage," mumbled Korb.

Su was familiar with Korb's musings at the denouement of a case. It generally meant that he knew who the culprit was but needed to figure out how to establish that conclusion to the satisfaction of the authorities. Korb hated to leave loose ends, which meant he probably wanted to determine the whereabouts of the explosive masks and tie them to Golden Dawn. Su wondered if where he had been this afternoon would help with that.

Korb abruptly lost his faraway look. His eyes focused on Su. "Here's what you need to do."

Chapter 33

KELAN SU

I needed to clear my head with a beach run and break a sweat. Blue Moon Beach was a stone's throw from our hotel. So I put on my black sports bra, black lycra shorts, black ankle socks, and my black running shoes. I had a small backpack over one shoulder. I'd probably deposit my shoes and socks there while running on the sand.

The day was clear and warm. The sun's rays were dazzling and hot in a cloudless azure sky. I slathered on the sunscreen and walked across the Gran Viale Santa Maria Elisabetta to the beach. A gentle breeze brought the salty scent of the Adriatic Sea wafting ashore. The water was a captivating deep blue, there were only a few people on the beach. Two other runners jogged past me.

I sat down in the warm sand, removed my shoes and socks and put them in my backpack. Standing up, I worked my toes into the sand. It felt good. I did some stretches and jogged in place for a few moments. With the prep and the warm sun, I was ready to get moving and find a smooth, comfortable stride on the flat, white sand beach.

I checked my watch–20 minutes out and 20 minutes back should be about five miles. Starting slow,

150 steps per minute, I gradually increased the stride to my usual 180. As the ground flowed by silently, my mind emptied of thought and filled with sensations. The warmth of the sun, the smoothness of the sand, the smell of the water, and the silky rolling of my muscles lubricated by sweat generated a kind of euphoria. Everything else melted away. I didn't notice if there was anyone else on the beach, although I'm sure I passed several other joggers. The sounds of voices, the light surf, and my breathing melded into a lyrical symphony.

When I finally glanced down at my watch, I had been running for 25 minutes. I arced around to head back. Looked like my run would end up a bit more than six miles.

When I reached my starting point, I was tired, but cleansed. The calm water looked inviting. I did have a towel, but the salt would wreak havoc with my spandex. *Oh, what the hell!* I ran into the warm but refreshing water. When I was up to my waist, I dove in, swam a few strokes and surfaced. Turning over on my back, I floated, bobbing in the light surf. The best way to end a run.

After a few minutes of luxuriating in the sea and sun, I walked back to the strand and toweled off. Heading back to the hotel shoeless, I was game for anything and pretty sure Korb's instructions would put my readiness to the test.

Chapter 34

KELAN SU

I wasn't sure how Korb was going to tie up this case, but it was clear what he wanted me to do. A drama had to be played out. I was his stage manager. He was both the director and the star. That suited me fine. I was accustomed to manipulating the supporting players onto their marks, choreographing their entrances and exits.

My first stop was Signor Giaccomo's office. I knocked on the dark mahogany door. It was so solid that my light rap barely made a sound. I knocked harder. Ouch! But that pounding elicited a response from within, a barely audible "*Entra!*"

I opened the door, admiring its smooth, silent swing despite the weight. The little man was sitting behind a huge mahogany desk over which I could only see his shoulders, neck, and head. He looked up at me and a broad smile lit up his face and his ruddy cheeks positively glowed.

I was taken aback at the evident pleasure he took in seeing me. "*Buongiorno,* Signor Giaccomo."

"*Buongiorno,* Signorina Su. What can I do for you?"

"Mr. Korb and I would like to use your large conference room, both sides, tomorrow afternoon. Say

181

from three to six. Is it available?"

"Let me see." Giaccomo turned to a computer screen on the right side of his desk and tapped on the keyboard. "No problem. It is available all day tomorrow. What do you plan to do?"

"Well, I hope you don't mind that we are going to confront some suspects in the case we are investigating?"

"Is it dangerous?" asked Giaccomo, his forehead wrinkling.

I thought he might be concerned and I was about to assure him that there would be a police presence. But then his eyes popped wide and he said, "Can I watch?"

"I think we can arrange that," I said, smiling at his excitement.

He picked up his phone, punched an intercom button, and told one of the hotel employees to meet him in the conference room. He got up and came around the desk. "Follow me."

The hotelier led me to a large, oak-paneled conference room, which was partitioned into two spaces by massive oak French doors. The thick glass panels in the doors were curtained to cut off the view of the opposite sides. He told Sergio, the young man whom he had called, to follow my instructions. Bowing slightly, still smiling, he left the room.

I oversaw Sergio's placement of chairs, assuring an adequately large and well-padded armchair with its back to the French doors for Korb and five less comfortable chairs facing Korb's in a semicircle. My chair, of intermediate comfort, observing protocol, was to Korb's right. Sergio flashed me some questioning looks, but responded quickly, "*Si, Signorina,*" to all my readjustment suggestions.

The partition was soundproof, but a CCTV system would allow those on the other side of the doors to hear and see what was happening on Korb's side. I asked Sergio to place four chairs facing the TV screen on the observers' side of the partition.

"Grazie, Sergio," I said, smiling fetchingly at him. For a moment, he looked at me intently. Then, turning hesitantly, he seemed uncertain where to find the door he must have entered or exited hundreds of times. I cursed myself insincerely for beginning to enjoy the effect I seemed to have on men.

My task now was to get Massimo, Porello, and Ibrahim to this meeting. Ibrahim was still in custody, so getting her there would be easy. Korb didn't want the two neo-fascists arrested as that would put any further investigation under the control of an examining magistrate. That would be surrender. His ego wouldn't stand for it.

I knew I'd need some canny tricks to get Massimo and Porello to come, but I had an idea on how to do this. Korb would take care of corralling Mia Strega, Chekova, and Tedesco. Of course, Mazzini and Campari would be there on the TV screen side with Giaccomo, Tedesco, and possibly Slobodan.

Chapter 35

After sending Su on her errands, Korb stared with hooded eyes at a stylized print of a tree on the opposite wall while contemplating his next move. While Su's task was daunting, Korb had the utmost confidence that she would succeed in bringing her charges to the hotel. He would have to get Mia Strega, Paola Chekova, and Tedesco to the confrontation. He took the easy one first.

Because of his debt to Vladimir Strega, Korb decided to approach Mia personally at her place of work and to let her father know what he was doing. He was able to convince Strega that allowing the detective to talk with Mia alone was in his daughter's best interests. Korb knew he would need to talk with Mia privately to drive home his point that her presence was necessary both for justice to be done and to save her own pretty neck. He also asked Strega not to warn the young woman of the meeting. Compliance with this request was less certain.

Once again, Korb overcame his reluctance to venture out onto the water. He called Treu to pick him up at the hotel dock. This would also keep Treu close and to allay any suspicions the officer might have that he was no longer trusted.

When Treu arrived twenty minutes later, the portly detective was waiting at the dock, trying to steel himself for his descent to the launch. Treu climbed the ladder and greeted Korb with a handshake. Korb nodded his head toward the boat. The officer grasped his meaning and turned back to the ladder. "I'll go part way down first and you can follow. That way I can guide you into the cockpit," he said with a tight smile. He might have been thinking of what would happen if Korb slipped and brought his 160 kilos down on top of him.

Korb grunted his assent and moved gingerly toward the ladder. Surprisingly, the boarding went off without a hitch and both men breathed a sigh of relief. However, Korb's relief was short-lived. The canal waters were rough, causing the boat to jump and buck like a wild mustang. Korb reached under his spread thighs to clamp a death grip on the hard plastic seat. He closed his eyes, but that made his feeling of loss of control worse. He fixed on a distant point that seemed to bounce less than foreground objects.

"Uh, where are we headed?" said Treu, hesitating to interrupt his passenger's struggle to get a hold of himself.

Korb slowly turned the seat toward the officer. "Murano, Calle Briati, just across from the Faro di Murano. Mia Strega works at Artevetro, a lighting design studio," croaked Korb. After he suppressed a belch that could have resulted in projectile vomit, he turned back to his fixed staring point.

Treu nodded with a slight smirk as he headed the launch into the chop. They were silent for the rest of the trip. The rising and falling lessened in the more open waters on the way to the island. By the time they pulled up to the dock, Korb had mastered his queasy stomach and was ready to confront Mia Strega.

Artevetro was spectacular, if not to Korb's more traditional taste. The room he entered from the street was large. The side walls were concrete blocks painted zinc white. The front wall was entirely glass. The back wall had thin aluminum strips standing out from a teak background. There were three doors set in the back wall. The ceiling was beamed in dark teak two-by-fours with white plaster sections between the beams. Hanging from the beams were perforated, slim, silver cylinders. From the perforations came twinkling LED lights and from the open ends a bright white light. The room was empty except for a receptionist seated in almost the exact middle at a teak table with curved, chrome legs. The blonde, white-clad receptionist with her long tanned legs fit right in with the ultramodern décor.

Korb walked slowly toward the young woman. "*Buongiorno*," he said, reaching up to remove his hat.

"*Buongiorno*, Signor. How may I help you?" asked the girl with a slight simper.

"I would like to see Miss Strega."

The receptionist frowned and looked at her iPad. "Do you have an appointment?"

"I don't, but I believe Miss Strega will want to see me," said Korb, staring hard at the girl. "Tell her Marko Korb is here to save her life."

The receptionist's head jerked up, her eyes widened, and her mouth dropped open.

"Tell her," the detective said firmly.

The girl's head gave one violent shake, and she lowered her eyes, saying nothing.

"Where is she?" barked Korb. The girl turned slightly and indicated the left-hand door with a motion of her head. She was shaking slightly.

Korb turned toward the door, but then looked back. "Get hold of yourself and tell Miss Strega I'm coming." His bottom lip protruded and his eyes took on a more sympathetic cast as he gazed at the woman. He turned back to the door, shaking his head.

Korb knocked once and opened the door. He was surprised to see an undecorated, strictly utilitarian workroom. Along one cement block wall were computer stations used for design work and viewing inventory. The rest of the room held worktables with several lighting fixtures in various stages of construction.

Mia Strega had just turned from her computer toward the door as Korb entered. She half rose from the chair and then plopped back down hard. Her shoulders sagged and her head lowered. "What do you want?"

Korb approached and glared at her. "I want to keep you out of jail, my dear. You will need to tell me the truth now about the night Pakulić was murdered. And you will need to tell it again tomorrow."

Strega's head swayed slowly from side to side and her chin lowered to her chest. She took a deep breath, exhaled, straightened her shoulders, and looked up at Korb, half defiant, half resigned. "All right, what do you want to know?"

Chapter 36

KELAN SU

We were again at the outdoor table across from Soledoro.

"Angela, wait here for me. If I'm not out in twenty minutes, call the cavalry."

"The cavalry?" Campari's brow furrowed.

"Oh, you know, the rescue squad, the *carabinieri*, the army."

"How about me and my Glock?" Angela said as her mouth twisted into a wry smile.

"Guess that'll have to do." I didn't know why I was reassured. There were probably several armed men in the shop with more to come once I said my piece.

Angela added, "Not to worry. I have HQ on speed dial."

I gave a short snort of a laugh at this.

As I crossed the cobblestone street, I considered my approach. A long shot, but my brief encounters with Massimo and Porello, and previous experience with macho thugs in Chicago, made me think it might work.

At the door, I stopped, took a deep breath, turned back to Angela, and sketched a wave. As I went in, a bell tinkled and there was the faint sound of a buzzer in another room. The showroom was empty. I heard voices and footsteps coming from the rear of the building. The first to appear was the clerk from our previous visits. His jaw dropped when he saw me. He turned to the man following him in.

I gave the trailer a bright smile. It was Porello. This played right into my plan. "I hope you've recovered from the beating I gave you. I try to go easy on pussies, but you did rip my brand-new dress."

Porello's eyes bulged. Despite his jowls, the cords in his neck stood out. His fists balled. The clerk heard the sharp intake of breath and turned toward him. He stared at Porello in amazement.

"Take it easy. I'm not going to hit you again. In fact, I came with a peace offering."

"Get outta here, bitch," blustered Porello.

"I can't do that, Fabio. I have an important message to deliver from Korb. You remember him. He's the guy who decked your tough guy enforcer."

"Sh-sh-ould I get Massimo?" the clerk asked querulously.

"Shut up!" Porello said through clenched teeth.

I could see the thug was trying to think of a way to rescue his manhood. It was time for the message. I changed to a more conciliatory tone. "Listen, I am trying to give you a heads up. We have enough evidence to turn over to the police. It ties you and Massimo to the time and place of Pakulić's murder as well as giving you a motive for the killing. But Korb doesn't really think you did it. He has an idea who did and expects that person to finger you."

The big man squinted at me. He couldn't seem to decide whether to listen or try and throw me out. The best he could come up with was, "So what?"

"Korb has arranged a little seance with these

witnesses. If you and Massimo come, you can find out what they have on you and confront them. At best, we will be able to show who really did the murder. At worst, you'll know what you need to prepare a defense against."

His eyes stayed narrowed, but one of his eyebrows lifted. I took that as a sign of interest. Time for another needle. "Of course, if you and your minion are afraid of being alone with me and Korb, I can assure you we won't get tough with you."

I tilted my head and pursed my lips, intending to convey sympathy for his lack of backbone. I hoped this would add up to a challenge they couldn't refuse. "So it would be wise for you and your colleague to come to the Hotel Lido at three tomorrow. Just the two of you–unarmed."

Porello frowned and grunted. "We'll think about it." But his fists had unclenched.

"Don't be late," I chirped, and turned back to the door. I looked at my watch–ten minutes. *This better work or Korb will have my head.*

Chapter 37

Korb had Treu drop him back at the hotel. He
didn't want the bent cop to be in on his next move.
Korb ordered a water taxi as soon as he entered his
suite. The taxi was to meet him at the hotel dock at 2:00
p.m., which gave him time for a light lunch. Light, for
Korb, meant only three courses.

He picked up his phone and punched in the number
for room service.

A voice answered, "*Si.*"

Korb ordered *baccalà mantecato*, a creamy puree
of dried salt cod served with polenta croutons, *spaghetti
al nero di seppia*, squid ink pasta, and two *tramezzini,*
sandwiches with assorted cheeses and Italian cold cuts.
This would be accompanied by a classic Venetian spritz
made with Prosecco, soda, and Aperol. He finished off
his order with an espresso.

Korb smacked his lips thinking of this repast.
While he waited, he sat in the large wing chair,
loosened his tie, kicked off his shoes, and put his feet
up on a hassock. He closed his eyes, rested his chins on
a closed fist, pursed his lips, and breathed deeply. He
was lost in thought when there was a knock at the door.
Quickly, he lowered his feet to the floor and
straightened his tie. For a moment, he thought of trying
to put his shoes on but realized it was hopeless.
"*Entra,*" he called.

The waiter appeared, pushing a squeaky wheeled cart laden with three covered dishes. Like Pavlov's dog, the squeak of the cart set off the gourmet's anticipation of the savory selections, and his mouth watered. The waiter moved the hassock and steered the cart over to Korb's chair. He indicated the order of the dishes, the pasta dish having a small lit sterno can underneath. The server poured the spritz from a carafe into a tall, iced flute and asked if he could do anything else. Korb signaled his satisfaction with the wave of a hand. The waiter nodded but did not move. Korb saw the check at the side of the table and signed it, adding a substantial tip. The waiter smiled, bowed his head deferentially, and backed out of the room, closing the door gently behind him. Korb sighed with a smile.

****

When the satisfied gentleman finished his espresso, he patted his lips daintily with a napkin, pushed the rolling table away, sighed, and propelled himself out of the chair with his arms. He stepped into his shoes. He had fifteen minutes to get down to the dock. He took stock of his options. Walking to an ornate dresser, Korb opened the top drawer. He took out a wad of bills, a business card, a torn slip of paper and a small notecard covered with densely packed script. Placing them in a little gift box, he sealed the box with an expertly tied piece of purple ribbon. He held the package out in front of him and smiled. He put the box in his pocket and closed the drawer. He glanced around the room peering as if looking for something hidden in the shadows. The detective shook his head almost imperceptibly and turned toward the door.

The water taxi was waiting when he reached the

dock. The driver was standing at street level ready to help his passenger in. Korb waved him away. Absorbed in thought, he stepped into the boat without hesitation or misstep. The boatman, jumping into the front of the craft, had to shout "*Signor, a dove?*" three times before Korb, his head finally snapping up and his eyes focusing on the young man, responded with his destination.

When the boat pulled over to a dock in the Dorsoduro sestiere on the Fondamenta delle Zattere, Korb noted that Chekova's pensione looked across at the Giudecca. "Wait here," he told the taxi driver. The man nodded with a frown. Korb mounted the steps to street level.

The area was rundown, right next to one of Venice's working ports. The boarding house was probably elegant years ago. It still had a rose-colored facade and Palladian windows, but the facade was pockmarked and some of the windows on the topmost floor had been boarded up.

Korb had two plans: one if Chekova was home, the other if she was not. He limped down the street leaning more heavily than usual on his cane. In addition to the constant dampness of Venice taking its toll on his old wound, he was not used to doing so much legwork.

There were three bare concrete steps up to the rooming house door. The door itself was a dark wood, the veneer peeling and splintering. It opened with a shriek into a foyer with buckling linoleum. There was a distinct odor of mold. A curving staircase to the right of the entrance would have been spectacular in its day. Now the steps were bare wood covered by rubber non-slip mats. The bannisters and newels were scarred and dull. To the left of the foyer was a plywood counter, and behind that was a wizened, bespectacled gnome whose head was just barely visible above the countertop. *If the man were standing*, Korb thought, *he couldn't be more than four feet tall.*

The fellow's thick glasses made his eyes appear like blue saucers. As Korb approached, the man glared at him and frowned. "What can I do for you?" he rasped in a surprisingly deep voice. It was not a tone that invited a request. *No matter*, thought Korb.

"What room is Signorina Chekova in? She's expecting me."

The clerk cocked his head and looked hard at Korb. "She's in room 310 to the right of the stairs."

Korb nodded and turned toward the stairs.

"But," the man interjected, "I'll save you a long climb. She's not in."

Korb turned slowly and stared hard at the miniscule clerk. He approached the counter again, nodding slowly. "Do you know when she might come back?"

"No."

"Do you know where she went?"

"No. What am I, her private secretary?"

Korb nodded again, a slight smile dawning on his face. He reached into his pocket and, with some difficulty, pulled out his wallet. Riffling through some bills, he pulled a few out and slapped them on the counter. "Would you be able to let me into her room? I have a little gift for her I am sure she will love." Korb reached into his other pocket and pulled out the small beribboned box.

The clerk looked at the box, then at the money on

the counter, and then lifted his head to Korb. He said nothing, nor did he move to take the money.

Korb nodded a third time. He dropped down several more bills.

This time the man smirked, swept up the cash and stuffed it into his pocket. He turned to the numbered cubbies behind him and reached into the one labeled 310.

The detective's surmise was confirmed—the clerk had been standing up. The little man ducked only minimally under a hinged section of the counter not bothering to raise it. He motioned to Korb to follow him. Heading toward the stairs, he glanced over his shoulder and said, "Watch that fourth step up, it's loose." He gave a snorty laugh.

Chapter 38

When Korb returned to his hotel room, he was ready to collapse into bed. The three-story climb, several boat rides, and unaccustomed leg work had wreaked havoc on the mammoth detective. Unfortunately, he had another task before he could bury himself under the covers.

He took out his cell phone and plopped into a large leather armchair. He tried to tap in Tedesco's number, but his thick and weary fingers kept missing the right numbers. He cursed mightily and slammed the cell down on a side table. With a massive exhale, he pushed himself up and shuffled over to a spindly, straight-backed, wooden chair that was next to a telephone table. Knees creaking, he lowered himself carefully into the chair whose creaking matched his own. He reached for the house phone and punched in Tedesco's number with only one mistake. The phone rang once, twice, three times. Korb was steaming to think of the effort he had wasted when a voice said, "*Pronto.*"

"Ah, Baron," Korb said.

A drawn-out, "Yesss," conveyed the suspicion characteristic of deadbeats receiving dunning calls.

"This is Marko Korb. Baron, I need your help."

"Yesss."

"We are winding up the Pakulić case."

"I hoped you would keep me out of this."

196

"You know that is impossible. Ibrahim is the key witness and you can corroborate her presence and ability to observe what happened."

"I don't want to be involved. What if I deny being there?"

"Come, come, sir. Ibrahim will say you were there. Others saw you with her. You would be looking at an obstruction of justice charge at the minimum if you lie about it."

There was a long silence at Tedesco's end.

"I have a proposition for you. I know you can no longer play bridge at the casino. The other players are tired of your unpaid losses and your masquerade as nobility."

There was a blustery growl at the other end of the line.

"Let's not quibble. You are desperate and living in a squalid little walk-up in the Giudecca. You even owe rent there. You come from Naples, not Venice, and your father was a butcher. Despite all the voice lessons, you still have a noticeable Southern accent. Everyone knows it."

"It's a lie. Where did you hear all this?"

"I am a detective, Tedesco, and you have a lot of folks at the casino who are happy to tear you down. But listen to me. You help me with my problem and I have a proposal that might help you."

"I'm listening."

Korb nodded and shifted the phone to the opposite ear. "There are two elderly British gentlemen who have been asking me to play some high-stakes rubber bridge. They think they are experts, but they are not. They want to play for one pound sterling a point. We can easily take them for a substantial sum."

"What's this got to do with me?"

"You'll be my partner."

"I can't handle those stakes."

"Losing more than you can pay wouldn't be new to you."

There was a long exhale from Tedesco's end.

"We are not going to lose as long as you follow my lead, simply describe your hand in the bidding, and drop your ridiculous aggressiveness. Play by the book. If we should lose, I will cover the losses."

"Why didn't you say that in the first place? But how do you know they aren't hustling us?"

Korb drummed his fingers on the telephone table. "I've checked, Tedesco. They have done this before and elsewhere. They usually win, but the competition has not been stellar. They play in their hotel room. I have already had someone look it over. No mirrors, peepholes, etc. We will have the cards delivered and dealt by the hotel management. They will agree because they know my reputation in the bridge world and want to beat someone at my level. They also know you are no winner."

"Okay. What do I have to do if I accept your proposal?"

"Tomorrow at two-forty-five sharp, you'll be at my hotel. We are confronting the suspects in the Pakulić case."

"W-wait a minute. I don't want to get involved with them. They're thugs and killers."

"Look, Baron. You are already involved. Ibrahim has put you at the scene. Anyway, you won't be part of the confrontation. All you need to do is be seen by

Ibrahim talking to one of the police officers who will be there. You don't need to say anything substantive. Just pass the time of day. What's important is that Ibrahim knows you are there and thinks you are telling all to the police. It'll keep her honest."

"Well, as long as you guarantee to keep me out of it."

Korb grimaced. "No guarantees. You really have no leverage to bargain. If you don't do this on your own, I will ask the police to pick you up as a material witness. If my plan is successful, however, you will most likely be relieved of any further responsibility in the case."

"I'll be there."

"Don't be late. You'll be talking to Detective Angela Campari. She'll identify herself to you. She already knows of your role and is with us on this plan."

There was another long exhale at Tedesco's end. "Right. If that's all, I need to go."

"That's all—until tomorrow. Goodbye."

There was a click at the other end.

Chapter 39

KELAN SU

"You know what you are to do, Kelan?" Korb removed his reading glasses and gave me a piercing look as he raised his head from his book.

"Yes, sir. When Angela brings in Ibrahim, she hands her off to me," I said in a matter-of-fact tone.

"And Tedesco?" Korb was relentless in checking details.

"He is to start talking with Campari while I delay bringing Ibrahim to the main room."

"Slivitz?"

"I cue Slivitz when Chekova arrives so she can glimpse him in the hallway talking to Signor Giaccomo. Then I escort Slobodan into the adjoining office where he can see and hear the confrontation without being seen."

"Right. Finally, you join me in the main room." Korb nodded with a half-smile.

The stage was set. As usual, Korb's stage directions were complex and I had to be on my toes. He liked these things to go off like clockwork. I couldn't help tapping my foot with impatience to get to work. Korb noticed.

He cocked his head to the right, looked at me obliquely, and frowned. "And you will be ready in case any of our major characters are reluctant to show up?"

I sighed. "Of course, sir. I have two of Inspector Mazzini's men ready to go with me to round them up. He has also assigned men to watch them should they try to leave town."

"Satisfactory. You may get on with it." He slipped on his glasses and picked up his book.

Whew!! Was I glad to get on with it!

****

Chekova stalked in, pushing past two hotel employees. She was early. Fortunately, Slivitz was too. Giaccomo wasn't around. I stepped up to Slivitz and tapped him on the shoulder. He turned, and I nodded toward Chekova steaming down the hall.

His eyes slid toward her for a moment, and he began a loud and earnest conversation with me. "Please tell Korb I am at his service in this matter."

"I will. He is counting on you."

Chekova couldn't help seeing and hearing us. She broke stride as she passed and gawked, recovered quickly and forged ahead. I turned to follow. "Ms. Chekova, Korb will be in the room to your right. He is expecting you." She must have heard because she turned toward the door on her right.

I had no time even for a breath as both Tedesco and Slobodan arrived just as the stout woman disappeared through the door. The entrances and exits began to resemble a Feydeau farce. I placed Tedesco on his mark in an obvious spot and showed Slobodan into an adjoining room that had a CCTV set up to view the confrontation. When I came back into the hall, Angela arrived with Ibrahim in tow. The girl's sullen expression changed to one of utter despair as she saw

Tedesco.

I nodded to Angela and she handed the girl over to me. Taking a firm hold on her arm, I muscled her into the room and seated her next to Chekova. The older woman looked over and started to rise, but I fixed her with a stern gaze and said, "Sit." She complied and scowled at Ibrahim.

I moved to the door to await the other arrivals. The next was Mia Strega and her father. Strega ushered his daughter by the elbow into the room.

I stepped between them, saying, "Sorry, just Mia." Strega's hands closed into fists and he seemed about to object. I added, "Korb will look out for her." Strega stepped back, and I directed the girl to the first chair with a hand at the small of her back. She sat, head down, shoulders slumped, hands clenched in her lap.

I had spent a restless night worrying that the main characters would not show. If they were half as smart as they thought they were, they would stay as far away from Korb as possible. But I needn't have worried. The two neo-fascists' attempts at swaggering entries were thwarted by a Laurel and Hardyesque collision and a labored squeeze through the door. The skinny Massimo freed himself first and edged into the room, sneering at me.

"Where's Korb?" he snarled.

"Signori, if you will please be seated, Mr. Korb will be here shortly," I said, giving them a Mona Lisa smile and a slight bow toward the two empty seats at the end of the row. There was an audible growl from Porello as he lowered himself into the chair. Massimo seemed more composed as he sat, leaning back and crossing his legs.

"We are waiting for one more—Signor Treu," I said.

"We were told no police," said Porello, half rising.

"He's not here in an official capacity. Korb thinks he might have something to tell us." I noticed Porello's eyes narrowing at the mention of Treu's possible contribution to our little performance.

A moment later, the officer came in, brow furrowed, and glanced around cautiously at the cast of characters. He hesitated momentarily before taking the empty seat between Strega and Ibrahim.

The room was silent except for the squeak and creak of the chairs as all the attendees fidgeted: Strega kneading her hands; Porello leaning forward resting his hands on his knees; Massimo trying to find just the right I-couldn't-care-less pose; Treu crossing his legs and tugging at his pants cuff; Ibrahim jerkily shifting her head and looking from side to side, and Chekova clenching and unclenching her teeth.

Standing slightly behind and to the side of the seated group, I fidgeted too, shifting my weight from leg to leg. The scene was set.

Seconds passed on this *tableau vivant* before Korb entered stage right, crossed to the large armchair facing the assembly, and lowered himself into it laboriously using both hands on the arms. I moved to a chair set up between Strega's end of the row and the doorway that gave me profile views of both my boss and the suspects, as well as allowing me to intercept anyone who tried to bolt for the door.

The large detective slowly surveyed the group. "Good afternoon, ladies and gentlemen," he said without an ounce of cordiality. "I am sure you are all a bit surprised at yourselves for accepting my invitation. But curiosity, the desire to gain intelligence, and the hope to show me up are strong motivations. So let us get down to business."

There were "hmmphs", sighs, and grumbles from the crew, which Korb took as agreement. Everyone's attention was now riveted on their interrogator.

"I am going to ask each of you some questions. I hope you will answer them frankly but lies and deception will also aid my quest. I have sources of information that allow me to evaluate your truthfulness."

Each of the group glanced suspiciously at those sitting beside them. Eying this, Korb fought the impulse to smile. But I could see the corner of his mouth twitch slightly in an upward direction. A good sign. He knew he had them.

Korb turned first to Mia Strega. He leaned in his chair and peered at her intensely. At first, she looked away toward the door, but then met his gaze. Her hands showed white knuckles as she gripped the sides of her chair. I only realized how quiet the room had become when Korb cleared his throat. It seemed like an explosion reverberating off the walls.

"Now, Miss Strega, I want you to tell me exactly what you did, saw, and heard in the early morning hours of May eleven when Stefan Pakulić was killed." The drama had begun.

Chapter 40

Strega took a deep breath and squared her shoulders. "Well, I was walking my dog, Tino, about two-fifteen a.m. Tino, that's short for Valentino," she began.

"Let's stick to the essential details," said Korb, giving her a slight smile.

"Yes, well, Tino had just done his business, and I turned to head home when I heard an argument. The voices seemed to come from around the corner of Rio Terra San Leonardo, and I was sure I heard the name Pakulić. I had heard that he was in Venice and up to no good. As you know, my family has had much grief at the hands of that man. My mother..." Strega exhaled and closed her eyes tightly.

Korb's lips pursed and his eyes half-closed as he gave Strega a moment before asking, "Were you aware of any details about why Pakulić was in Venice?"

"Only that the Bosnian expat grapevine had it that he was working with Golden Dawn on some kind of action against our community."

"Okay. You heard the voices and the name. What did you do next?"

"I was torn. Should I go back and get my father? But I had a pistol in my purse that my father had given me for protection. We live in a rough neighborhood. I pulled it out. I must have dropped Tino's leash then."

"Is your pistol a Walther P22?" asked Korb.

"I don't know. It's small. My dad said it was a twenty-two."

"What were you going to do with the pistol?"

"I don't know. I wasn't thinking straight, but I really wanted to confront Pakulić. My heart was filled with hate. I guess I wanted to kill him, but only after I reminded him of what he had done to my family."

"What did you do then?"

"I followed the voices to where Pakulić, two other men, and a woman were standing along the canal on the rio terra."

"Did you recognize any of those people?"

"I had no idea who the woman was. But I knew what Pakulić looked like and I recognized Massimo and Porello from pictures I had seen in the papers."

There was nervous shifting among those who were identified. Massimo shook his head vigorously. Porello slapped his hands against his knees. Chekova turned her head away from Strega. She knew what question was coming next.

"And are any of the people you saw on the rio terra that night, or should I say early morning, here today?"

Strega turned toward the right and leaned forward. Massimo and Porello, who were staring at her, quickly turned their heads away. Too late, of course.

"Yes," she said. "The person sitting to the right of the young woman is Tiziano Massimo and to his right is Fabio Porello. The woman down at the end of the row of chairs is the woman I saw on the rio terra that night."

Korb paused his questioning to let the IDs sink in. The detective closely watched the reactions of the people named. The eyes of all three opened wide and mouths gaped, but only momentarily. They each made successful efforts to recompose their expressions, but jaw lines and blanched cheeks indicated clenched teeth.

Porello interjected, "Damnable lies! She already admitted that she came to kill Pakulić."

Korb glared at Porello. "Silence. You will get your chance to respond. Is it not to your advantage to hear the story out and know what may be raised against you?"

Strega leaned back in her chair, hoping that her questioning had ended, but the interrogator was not done with her.

"Now, Miss Strega, what happened next?"

For a moment, Strega seemed about to speak, but the words caught in her throat. She gave a little cough and said, "I-I stepped up to Pakulić and pointed the gun at him. I said 'You bastard. You killed my mother.' But my hand was shaking so much that Pakulić must have realized I couldn't pull the trigger. He laughed and slapped the gun out of my hand. It fell to the ground and went off. I don't think the shot hit anyone, but I panicked at the sound and ran off."

"Can you tell me how the parties were lined up when you arrived on the scene?"

"Well, let me see. Pakulić was directly in front of me with his back to the canal. I think Massimo and Porello were directly behind me facing Pakulić, and that woman there was to my right about four meters away."

"After the gun went off, all of the people you identified were still there in the same relative positions as when you first encountered Pakulić?"

"Yes, I think so, but I was in turmoil and my eyes

were blurred with tears."

"Did you hear a second shot?"

"No, I was running away. My ears were ringing from the first shot. All I could hear was my own panting and the clack of my heels. Oh, yes, and I think I heard Tino barking."

"Did you go straight home?"

"Yes. Tino must have seen me running home and followed me."

"Is there anything you wish to add, Miss Strega?" said Korb with a slight smile and a nod of his head.

"Just that I wanted to kill Pakulić. I couldn't, but I'm glad someone did."

"Understandable. Thank you, Miss Strega, for your full cooperation. Please remain seated to hear what the others have to say. We may solicit your comments on their statements," said Korb, again with the momentary half smile and nod toward Strega. The young woman seemed to take these gestures as signs of approval and leaned back in her chair, letting out her bated breath.

****

Korb's gaze swung past Treu and Ibrahim and fixed on Massimo. The wiry thug attempted to return the detective's penetrating stare but could only hold the gaze for a moment before lowering his eyes.

"Now, Signor Massimo, your take on what happened that night on the rio terra? Don't bother denying your presence there with Pakulić. There are too many witnesses and pictures that place you with the victim and at the scene."

Massimo closed his eyes and rubbed the back of his neck. He mumbled something under his breath that sounded like "you fat bastard." He scowled at Korb, his lips pinched in a tight line. He looked to Porello, who pursed his lips and shook his head. Stonewalling was clearly on Massimo's mind. But when Korb said, "Do you really think your colleague wants you to explain why you couldn't have killed Pakulić?" Massimo's resolve faded.

The interrogator moved quickly to exploit his advantage, knowing that Massimo was not particularly bright. "You and Porello brought Pakulić to that spot to confront him about his failure to deliver what he promised, didn't you?"

Massimo exhaled. "We just wanted to talk to him."

"About the aid that had not been delivered? Don't deny it. We have his letter offering assistance," Korb pressed on.

"Y-yes.He had made us some promises that had not been kept."

"That would give you a pretty good motive for murder, Signor Massimo. We have motive and opportunity. We also have pictures showing you and Porello dragging him out of the Casino."

"No, no, no. We did want to confront him and beat him up, but he showed us documents confirming the arrival of the assistance in ten days. We didn't kill him. We had no reason to then."

Porello started to rise. "Shut up, you imbecile," he hissed. Su had moved around behind him, placing her hands on his shoulders and pushing him down in his seat. He struggled against Su's grip to no avail.

"Tiziano, we know that the promised assistance was explosives, specifically C4 or plastique. But when the mask shop was raided, the explosives were not there. You will have to produce them before I or the police will accept your story," said Korb.

"You are fucking selling us down the river, you dumb shit," yelled Porello.

"I'm not taking the rap for any murder," Massimo yelled back to Porello. Turning to Korb, he said, "I got nothin' more to say. I don't know about any explosives."

"Gentlemen, gentlemen, this is getting us nowhere," said Korb, but his bemused smile and raised eyebrows did little to conceal his interest in the exchange. "Your motive for killing Pakulić may have become less certain. But you still had the best opportunity. The gun was lying on the ground in front of you."

"B-but it was Pakulić who told us to go after the girl and bring her back. He wanted to find out what she had heard and probably to smack her around a bit. He enjoyed that sort of thing," said Massimo. "Both Porello and I took off after her, but she got away. When we returned, the rio terra was empty."

"When you took off after Miss Strega, who was still there at the rio terra?" said Korb.

Massimo glanced quickly at Chekova, who was looking away. "Pakulić and Chekova," he said.

Korb closed his eyes and nodded. "Was the pistol still on the ground?"

"I think so. Pakulić hadn't moved to pick it up."

"Did you hear a second shot?" asked Korb.

"I don't know. Maybe. I heard something that could have been a shot. But we were running hard and couldn't hear much but our own steps. Porello was shouting about which way he thought the girl had gone."

"You said that when you returned to the rio terra, no one was there. Whom did you expect to find?"

"Yes. But no one was there."

"Whom did you expect to find?"

"Pakulić and Chekova."

"No one else?"

"No. Who?"

"Did you know where Pakulić and Chekova went?"

"Well, I guess Pakulić was in the drink," said Massimo with a short, nervous laugh. "Don't know about Chekova. She must have lit out after—"

"After what, Signor Massimo?" said Korb leaning forward, his left eye half closing.

"Uh. After whatever happened. I wasn't there. I don't know."

"Now, Signor Massimo, do you know of any reason why Signorina Chekova would want to kill Pakulić?"

"No, but she never had anything good to say about him. She was always trying to convince us not to deal with him. I got the feeling that she hoped we would rough him up. It seemed personal."

Chekova turned to Massimo with fiery hatred in her eyes. "You are a spineless, stupid, lying stooge."

Su quickly moved behind Chekova to restrain her if necessary. It was not. Chekova turned away, shaking her head.

Su thought, *Massimo better watch his back. Chekova certainly believed that "revenge was a dish best-served cold."*

Chapter 41

As Korb turned away from him, Massimo, who had been on the edge of his chair, sagged against the chair back with a sigh. The room was getting warm and the stink of sweat was rising. The detective had intentionally kept the AC off and the windows closed. This was all part of the close and pressured environment he wanted to create. Yet despite his rolls of fat, double-breasted suit, tightly knotted tie and the tension in the room, Korb was cool and dry.

The detective's gaze traveled to Porello, who met his stare with teeth clenched, his jaw muscles distinctly outlined. There were beads of sweat on the neo-fascist thug's bald pate and his face and neck were red.

"Signor Porello," said Korb, "do you have any additions or corrections to your colleague's description of events?"

"I have nothing to say to you, you interfering kike," said Porello, his mouth twisted in a toothy sneer. He crossed his left leg over his right and twisted in his chair, looking away from Korb and staring at the wall.

"Now, now, Signor Porello, let's not be childish. Your colleague has told us things that would support a claim that neither you nor he killed Pakulić. Don't you want to back him up?"

Still not looking at Korb, Porello said, "My colleague, as you call him, is a coward and a fool. I am not obliged to claim my innocence here."

"If you wish, I can call in Chief Inspector Mazzini, who may also call an examining magistrate. There is enough evidence for a formal charge of murder. As you know, that will open you to immediate detention, seizure of your business records, and all manner of searches and interrogations. Is that what you want?"

Porello pulled from his pants pocket a large white handkerchief and began to mop his head and face. *A sign of surrender?* thought Korb.

"All right, Su, will you call in the Chief Inspector."

Porello turned to Korb. "Just a minute. What guarantees do I have that if I verify Massimo's account, you won't call the cops anyway?"

"There are no guarantees. Everything depends on how fully and honestly you answer my questions. But if you do so, I give you my word that I won't turn you over to the police to face the charge of murdering Pakulić. I am known to be a man of my word."

One side of Porello's mouth turned up into a tight, wry expression. He nodded slightly. "Okay. Massimo, Chekova, and I did bring Pakulić from the Casino to the rio terra to confront him, but he convinced us that the aid he promised would be delivered. The girl with the gun was there as Massimo said and Pakulić disarmed her causing a shot to be fired. He then sent us after the fleeing girl. We did not hear a second shot, as we were running. When we returned, no one was there on the rio terra, and the gun was also gone. That's all I'm going to say."

"If that's all, then you haven't earned my help in avoiding a murder charge. Where the explosive masks now?"

Porello grunted and shook his head once.

Korb compressed his lips and slowly shook his head as well. He uttered an annoyed *tsuh*. "I have one more question," he said, pointing to Treu. "How did you know this man was a police officer?"

"What?" said Porello, shaking his head, clearly caught off balance by the question. Treu, also surprised, made to rise from his chair. Catching himself, he settled back down trying to look unconcerned.

"When this man entered the room, you said 'I thought you said no police.' You knew he was an officer."

Porello hesitated. "I don't know. I must have seen him around and someone told me he was a cop."

Korb nodded at Su. She clicked a remote and a monitor next to Korb lit up with the casino security cam picture that showed Massimo, Porello, and Chekova seeming to congratulate a smiling Officer Treu.

"What was the occasion for this show of approval for the officer?"

Porello said nothing. His eyes narrowed and his lips compressed into a tight line.

Korb turned to Treu, who was leaning forward, hands on knees, staring at the picture. "Can you explain this, sir?" the interrogator barked. "And can you explain why this and other incriminating casino security pictures were not mentioned in your report to Inspector Mazzini?"

Treu's jaw dropped. He slumped back in his chair, exhaled loudly, and looked down at the floor to his right. "I have nothing to say," he muttered.

"Before I turn you over to Inspector Mazzini and suggest that you be charged with accessory to murder, you might want to answer a few questions. They could save you from the more serious charge," suggested Korb, glowering at the officer. "For instance, how long have you been a member of Golden Dawn?"

Treu shook his head, still looking down. When he looked up at Korb, he stammered, "Th-that's not illegal."

"When it includes interfering with a police investigation and covering up evidence of a murder, it is. However, those charges are less devastating than complicity to a murder."

"Okay, okay. I did warn Porello about the police raid and I failed to report the pictures, but I had nothing to do with the murder. I wasn't anywhere near the casino or the crime scene when Pakulić was killed."

"While that's hard to believe, it can be checked with casino security and our other witnesses. However, an important show of good faith would be for you to tell us where the masks were taken and where they are now."

"I don't know exactly where they were taken or where they are now," whined Treu. "But I heard Porello say they were taken to an abandoned building on an isolated island. I don't know which one."

Porello glowered at Treu, bared his teeth, and hissed, "*Traditore.*"

Korb turned to Su. "Take Officer Treu and these two 'gentlemen' to Inspector Mazzini and tell him what we have learned," said Korb, indicating Porello and Massimo. "Ask him to take them into custody, allowing no phone calls or contact with others. Tell him we will soon be giving him the name of the murderer. Get back here as soon as you can."

"A man of his word!" hissed Porello.

"Imbecile. If you escape a murder charge, it will be thanks to me," said Korb through clenched teeth.

Su nodded. She moved to the door ahead of the threesome, who had arisen and were trying to get out quickly. Su opened the door. With a wave of her hand and a nod, she signaled Mazzini and Campari that they were to approach and waited for them to escort Porello, Massimo, and Treu out, followed them, and closed the door behind her.

Ibrahim seemed rooted in her seat, chewing her lips, eyes wide and glazed, white-knuckled hands gripping the arms of the chair. As Korb's gaze passed over her toward Chekova, the girl whimpered. Chekova was preparing to rise. The detective's eyes bore down on her. She fell back in her seat.

Just then Su opened the door and entered. She nodded to her boss. Korb made a sideways motion with his head. Su moved behind Chekova's chair.

"Ms. Chekova, I think you had better stay seated and listen to these next questions. Vice-Consul Slivitz is in the next room and may have something important to tell you."

Korb turned to Ibrahim. She was looking at Chekova, her arms tightly wrapped around herself. She was shivering.

"Ms. Ibrahim, if you answer my questions truthfully this time, you may avoid serious trouble."

A soft, high-pitched whine escaped her torn lips. "W-What do you want?"

"You were at the scene of the Pakulić murder longer than you originally told us."

Ibrahim looked down, shaking her head.

"Tell us what you were doing and who you were with at the time of the murder."

"You know that already."

"We need to hear it again, step by step. Convince us that you are telling the truth this time."

She nodded, not looking up. "I was with a trick. He's out there in the hall."

"You mean the Baron?"

"Yes, that's what he calls himself."

"Did he stay with you all the time you were watching the scene?"

"No. He was so scared he peed himself. He scooted when we heard the shouting–the pussy."

"So it must have seemed, but he stopped and hid behind the corner of a nearby building. He's right outside so we can check up on your story," said Korb.

Ibrahim frowned. "I thought I saw him crossing the road when I lit out."

"Okay. What did you see and hear before the first shot?"

"Well, I told you. I first saw three men and two women. Two of the men and the women had their backs to me. One of the women was off to the side, on my right. The other was standing between two men and Pakulić, who was facing me. The woman, the younger one, facing Pakulić was yelling at him in Serbo-Croatian, my language, calling him a bastard and saying he had murdered her mother."

"How far away were you from the group at this time?"

Ibrahim shook her head and grimaced. "I don't know. I'm not good at distances, especially with one eye."

217

"Well, Mineta, this room from the door to the far wall is about nine meters. About how many of these room lengths were between you and Pakulić?"

The girl looked from the door to the wall, then up at the ceiling with her eyes closed and her lower lip over her top lip. "About three times the length of this room."

"And there was enough light to identify the parties?"

"Yeah. There was a full moon along with a couple of streetlights."

"Okay. What did you see and hear next?"

"I saw the girl point what looked like a gun at Pakulić. Everyone except him seemed frozen. He laughed and stepped up to the girl. He slapped the gun out of her hand. It went off when it hit the ground. The shot must have gone wild. I didn't see anyone act like they were hit."

"And then?"

"The girl gave a loud cry and ran off. Pakulić said something I didn't catch and the two other men ran off after the girl. The bastard then said something to the older woman. She moaned, more like a grunt really, and reached over to pick up the gun that had landed close to her. Pakulić went for her. He called her a scruffle, no, a scrofulous, disgusting cunt. She screamed. It was unearthly. And then she fired. He staggered back and fell into the canal."

Chekova tried to rise, but was forced back down in her chair by Su's pressure on her shoulders. She screamed, "You lie, you slut."

Ibrahim shook her head vehemently. "No."

"Go on, Mineta," said Korb. "What happened

next?"

"I don't know. I turned and ran as fast as I could until I was out of breath. I sat down on the street with my back against a wall. Then I realized that the beast finally got what was coming to him." She gave Chekova a sad-eyed, almost sympathetic, look. "Only wished I had done it myself and he had suffered more."

"Thank you, Ms. Ibrahim. I am convinced that you have now told us the truth. I will make your help known to Inspector Mazzini. He may, of course, need you at a later date as a witness. Please go and report to Detective Campari. She is right outside."

Ibrahim slowly nodded and released a heavy sigh. She rose from the chair and trudged out of the room in unsteady steps.

Chapter 42

The room was sweltering. Even the walls were sweating. Chekova's light summer blouse showed dark rings under the arms. Su, still looking cool, noticed that sweat was running down the back of the woman's neck. A slightly sour odor rose from her. Korb's intense gaze resting on Chekova upped the temperature. The stocky woman was clearly melting.

She gave a quick shake of her shoulders trying to gather her strength. "Nothing but lies," she murmured. She tried to glare back at Korb.

The detective let out a deep breath, his head slanting sideways as he looked at the woman. "All right, Paola. You may continue to deny what has been said here. But I think that the Italian authorities can make a very convincing case against you."

Chekova sobbed. Her last ounce of bravado fading.

"As I have promised from the beginning, if you deal fairly with me, I can help. I sympathize with you. I know that bastard Pakulić treated you abominably. I would hate to see the person who put an end to that rabid animal sent to prison," Korb said softly, almost soothingly. He did both good cop and bad cop himself.

Chekova's mouth opened and brows lifted in an almost hopeful look. That was replaced almost immediately with a scowl and shake of her head.

"So you can go to court here on a charge of

murder. Oh, maybe you can say you feared an attack or had provocation and get the charge reduced somewhat, but you will still do time. Or you can help me and the Italian authorities put an end to the threat of a terrorist attack planned by Pakulić and Golden Dawn. After all, you always intended to foil Pakulić's plans."

Korb paused, lips pressed into a hard, straight line and brow furrowed. Chekova leaned back in her chair, eyes tightly shut, the possibilities sinking in. Su's head cocked to the right and a small smile dawned on her chiseled features.

Korb went on. "Vice-Consul Slivitz is here to assure you that he can put you on the consular protocol list giving you diplomatic immunity in Italy and that he will give you credit back home for preventing a Serbian connection to a major international incident."

The woman's cheeks ballooned as her face twisted and tensed. Then she let out a long breath. "What do you want me to do?" she said in a low rasp.

"First, you must tell us where the explosive masks are being stored," said Korb. Chekova's hand went to her mouth and her eyes narrowed as she looked past the large detective.

"Don't quibble. We know you were privy to that information."

The woman frowned. "I want to see Slivitz. He needs to confirm the deal."

The large detective sighed. He nodded to his aide-de-camp. Su removed her hands from the back of Chekova's chair and strode to the door. She ushered Slivitz in. The diplomat frowned as he looked at Korb, who had his hands clasped under his nose and was regarding the ceiling. When the Vice-Consul turned toward Chekova, she gave a slight, sheepish smile and dropped her head. Slivitz cleared his throat. Korb snapped to as he noticed the diplomat.

"Bogodan, I'm sorry to have to call you in, but Ms. Chekova needs confirmation that you can and will add her name to the Cerionline diplomatic protocol list for the mission."

The tall, stooped diplomat pressed his lips tightly closed, and looked from Korb to Chekova, whose head was now up, her eyes wide, and her mouth open. He nodded. "I have set it up. I just need to call it in."

"Thank you, Bogodan. When I get the information I am seeking and it is checked out, I will let you know to make the call. Ms. Chekova, I think you also owe Vice-Consul Slivitz thanks and me an answer to my question."

The woman nodded and took a deep breath. "Well, you understand that I wasn't really privy to any plans or decisions about the explosives or about any actions Golden Dawn was planning. In fact, I was trying to discourage them from working with Pakulić." Her voice had taken on a high-pitched, lisping tone–innocent as a young girl.

"Yes, yes," murmured Korb impatiently. Slivitz glowered and shook his head. He nodded once to Korb and left the room. Su returned to her position behind Chekova's chair.

"But Porello and Massimo weren't careful about discussing their plans. They seemed to forget I was around. They mentioned a deserted, off-limits island with a huge, closed, and broken-down psychiatric hospital. It had a frightful reputation for sadistic experiments and was rumored to be cursed, which also served to keep people away. There were still several mostly intact rooms with barred doors and windows."

"Kelan, can you call in Inspector Mazzini and please turn on the air conditioning," said Korb with a satisfied smile. Su returned his smile and left the room.

"You said no police," Chekova rasped breathlessly.

"Listen, Paola, Inspector Mazzini will have to check out this island. It sounds like Poveglia in the lagoon. If he finds the masks, our deal holds. If not…" Korb raised his left arm from the elbow, palm up, cocking his head and raising his eyebrows. The stocky woman shuddered, acknowledging both the threat and the startup of the AC.

"There is one other thing. You'll have to give the Inspector a signed statement detailing what you know about Porello, Massimo, and Golden Dawn's connection to the masks as well as Pakulić's activities and death."

Mazzini entered the room followed by Su. "Ah, Inspector, the explosive masks are in one of the patient cages on Poveglia. I think you'd better get an explosives team out there right away. It would be good if you would accompany them. We don't want them disappearing again. Let me know as soon as you find them."

"Yes, Signor Korb," said Mazzini, and he turned on his heel.

"A moment, Inspector. Signorina Chekova has agreed to give you a full written statement about the connections between Porello, Massimo, Golden Dawn, Pakulić, and the masks. This is something you should probably only share with your most trusted colleagues." The large detective looked hard at the woman and she nodded once. Mazzini gave her a glance, turned back to Korb, and also nodded. He turned again and strode to the door.

"Kelan, will you take this lady out and keep an eye on her. She may need to freshen up. Perhaps Detective Campari has returned and can assist you. Also, make sure Porello, Massimo, and Treu are in custody and, for the moment, incommunicado. You can tell the others to leave."

Su couldn't keep herself from saluting Korb and saying, "Right, Chief." She didn't know exactly how, but he had done it again, seemingly wrapping up all the loose ends. Now it was up to the Italian authorities. She and Korb could go home.

The young woman helped the older woman out of her chair with a light grip on her elbow. The woman staggered for a moment and was a bit unsteady on her feet. Once Chekova steadied herself, Su gently urged her toward the door.

When they had left, Korb laboriously stood up. Straightening his jacket and pants crease, he looked once from one end to the other at the row of chairs. Then he looked into the distance and smiled.

Epilogue

KELAN SU

"*Cin! Cin!*" chorused a gaggle of voices as flutes lifted. The sparkling Prosecco was imbibed, lips smacked, and smiling, congratulatory faces looked to Korb, who was standing at the head of a table laden with *amuse-geule*. We were in the hotel's terrazzo courtyard lined with fan palms. Mazzini was on his right and I on his left. Angela, LuLu, Chef Alberti, Signor Giaccomo, Strega and his daughter, Slivitz, Slobodan, and two of his homeless friends were present, the latter fidgeting and looking hungrily at the delicious tidbits.

The Prefect and the Chief of the Venice Police were also present, standing stiffly at the rear of the room, hands clasped behind their backs. They were not among the smiling onlookers. These gentlemen were chagrined by the ties to Golden Dawn of several police officers that had been discovered by Korb and Mazzini. It was not entirely clear where these officials' sympathies lay.

In truth, my smile was not because of the success of our endeavor as much as relief that we would be heading home. I was also glad to pay my debt to LuLu by including him in this gathering. His smile was directed more at me than my boss.

There was a tinkling of glass echoing throughout the room. I looked across Korb's bulk and saw the Inspector stepping forward and tapping his glass with a small fork from the table. He cleared his throat and turned slightly toward the great detective.

"Signor Korb, my congratulations and extreme gratitude for the brilliant and expeditious way you helped us clear up Pakulić's murder and prevented a disastrous terrorist attack." Mazzini lifted his glass again. "I would like to propose a toast to you, and of course, Signorina Su." He looked across my boss and nodded to me. His smile, one eyebrow raised, was slightly libidinous, which sent an electric shock traveling down my spine. He turned back to the audience and put the glass to his lips. The assembly uttered, "*Si, si,*" as they sipped again.

"I would like to add that all of the explosive masks have been accounted for and turned over to the military. The leaders of Golden Dawn are in custody and are vying to rat each other out. Paola Chekova who shot Pakulić fearing he was about to attack her was protected by diplomatic immunity. She has been expelled from Italy. In reality, she did us a big favor, forestalling the terrorist attack, locating the explosives, and leaving us a sworn statement connecting Golden Dawn to the plot."

I was grateful for Mazzini's abbreviated recounting of the events of the last two days. So were our guests who were shifting from foot to foot looking from the food to the bar where refills of Prosecco were to be had.

Mazzini asked Korb whether he would like to say a few words. The large man nodded. There was a stifling of sighs from the group. Mine took the form of a long exhale. I needn't have worried. The detective sensed and shared the desire of everyone to move on to the delicacies.

He said, "I want to extend my congratulations to Inspector Mazzini and the Venice police for their efficiency in resolving this matter. Thank you all for coming. Thanks also to Signor Giaccomo and Chef Alberti for the delectable spread, excellent quaff, and exceptional hospitality. Please dig in." Eyebrows raised, Korb and I exchanged relieved smiles.

I filled my plate and stepped over to the bar to get another glass of bubbly. I listened vaguely to the murmur of voices and watched as most of the guests approached Korb to shake his hand. The police brass were the first, solemnly giving Korb that European one up and down handshake and tight smiles. They left immediately. Strega embraced him warmly and Mia hesitantly offered him her hand and half-smiled with her eyes downcast. Angela came over to me and we hugged. I would miss her. We promised to stay in touch. LuLu took my hand and kissed it. He thanked me profusely for inviting him and introducing him to "the great detective."

"I hope you will return soon to Venice. I would love to show you its hidden treasures. You are the most charming young woman, despite our brief acquaintance, that I have ever met," he said. We both blushed.

Having finished the second glass of Prosecco, I was euphoric. No loose ends. Our bags were packed and our flight home was booked for that evening.

A word about the author...

Lawrence E. Rothstein is a retired lawyer and university professor who has published in constitutional law, privacy law and labor law. He was born and raised in Chicago and since 1974 has resided with his wife and family in beautiful southern Rhode Island. He has lived and traveled widely in Europe. An avid reader of detective fiction, Rothstein has always wanted to write detective novels. *Venetian Bind* is his first novel of a prospective series involving the corpulent detective, Marko Korb, and his Chinese-American, right-hand woman Kelan Su. Together they form an unbeatable sleuth duo that will keep readers on the edge of their seats.

For more information on Korb and Su and their exciting exploits as well as recipes and wine pairings from the novel, please visit and register on: www.Rothsteinsmysteries.com